EIGHT DARK RIDERS

Noah S Wallace

EIGHT DARK RIDERS

BY

NOAH S WALLACE

Illustrated by
Isaiah Wallace

A Harbinger House Book

Harbinger
House BOOKS

Apprehending Truth Publishers
Cookeville, Tennessee

Eight Dark Riders is a work of fiction. Any resemblance to actual persons, living or dead is purely coincidental. Biblical application herein is completely accurate to the best of the authors understanding.

Harbinger House Books is an imprint of:
Apprehending Truth Publishers
P.O. Box 692 | Cookeville, Tennessee 38503 USA
www.atpublishers.com

Book & cover design by PureLight Graphics
Illustrations by Isaiah Wallace

ISBN: 978-0-9886253-9-6

First Edition

22 21 20 19 / 10 9 8 7 6 5 4 3 2
190819

EIGHT DARK RIDERS

1

Thick, stormy clouds hid the bright light of the full moon, on that dreary July night of 1874. Outside of the small town of Burlington, Wyoming; a dark and enormous thunderhead cracked over the prairies and woods. An occasional streak of lighting lit up the storm-clad night. The wind was howling, and the thunder cracked over the small town in sudden, reverberating claps. That dismal night held fear and dread, whose shadows told of an evil tale; a story of eight dark riders. Their ghostly appearance was mean and terrifying. Lined up in a row, they stood as black and grim silhouettes against the storm lit sky, and they silently sat in their saddles, being drenched in the torrent of rain, examining the valley below.

Down in the valley, there was a small log house; a fire glowed in the fireplace suggesting that the house was occupied. The Cassidy family had just sat down to dinner. None gathered round the lowly table seemed to notice the fierce, howling winds that beat against the house, for all assumed safe, comfort and ease. All were present at the dinner table: Father, Marie who was eighteen, little James, and little brother Pete who had just turned three. Their mother had died three years before; the sorrows of their loss faded slowly through the years. But in this night, sorrows would begin afresh, that is for Little James, who was only nine years old.

The supper was tasty. It was the good old-fashioned chicken and dumplings, with dinner rolls, and spearmint tea. Marie had learned much from her mother, not the least of which was attested by the table's appetizing spread. The dinner table was unusually quiet; the clatter of forks and spoons on metal plates were the only sounds heard above the din of the storm. Every now and then, they would glance towards the curtain draped window, as a streak of lighting lit up the candle-lighted room.

After they had all finished their meal; Father remained at the table, while Marie picked up the dinner dishes. It was his way to read from the Bible to the family, while they did their inside chores. Father took the big, aged and worn Bible from off the fireplace hearth and opened it to where he had his marker. Pete played with his toys on the floor under Father, as he read...

With the pure thou wilt shew thyself pure; and with the froward thou wilt shew thyself froward. For thou wilt save the afflicted people; but wilt bring down high looks. For thou wilt light my candle: the LORD my God will enlighten my darkness. For by thee I have run through a troop; and by my God have I leaped over a wall. As for God, his way is perfect: the word of the LORD is tried: he is a buckler to all those that trust in him.

For who is God save the LORD? or who is a rock save our God? It is God that girdeth me with strength, and maketh my way perfect. He maketh my feet like hinds' feet, and setteth me upon my high places. He teacheth my hands to war, so that a bow of steel is broken by mine arms. Selah.

James evening chore was to go to the next room adjoining both the porch and kitchen, and get firewood brought in and stacked for the next day's warmth. *'He teaches my hands to war, so that a bow of steel is broken by mine arms.'* That verse sounded so charming to his young mind; he had a small childish thought that one day maybe his hands could war.

While he had been meditating on the passage his Father had read, they heard many horses coming to the front door; clipping and clopping on the wet ground. The storm had subsided to a drizzle; which made the sound of the horses' hooves on the saturated ground even more distinct. They heard the neighing of many horses and the sound of men talking. James peered over a large pile of firewood into the living room where his father and sister were.

"It's a group of riders, and they don't look friendly." Marie stated, pulling the curtains away from the window and peering out.

James left his wood pile and started walking to his Father to see these bizarre looking visitors, clothed in black. Father stepped up, fastened on his gun-belt, and then opened the door. But before he could even greet them, or ask them their business, they shot him down right where he stood. James' father grabbed his chest and fell to the floor, four bullets had gone through him. James stared at his father, the realization of what just happened had not sunk in.

In total horror and shock, James screamed out, "Daddy!" He turned back around and ran and hid behind the wood pile he had been stacking and watched in fear and disbelief. Screaming, Marie grabbed little Pete and ran for the back bedroom; but before she slammed the door and locked it, she looked back toward where James was hiding. She tried to decide in that moment whether she had the time to go get James, but a look towards the door convinced her otherwise. With tears in her eyes, she threw him a kiss with a wave of her hand and secured the door, knowing that he would be safer in hiding than for her to reveal his presence. That last gaze he saw in his sisters' blue eyes engraved an image in little James' mind; an image he would always bear with him till his dying day.

The men started to beat on the bedroom door; but before long, the door could not hold back their heavy onslaught, and it burst open. Wood splintered, and the heavy door fell with a crash as the evil men plunged their way in. James shuddered, for it seemed as if the heavy thunder and the crashing of the bedroom door sung a ghostly song in wicked rhythm and ghostly harmony. But to the intruder's shock and to James' surprise; Marie had one of her fathers' pistols and shot five rounds from the Colt Peacemaker into the men, killing two of the outlaws.

They retreated behind the walls and tried to convince her to throw her gun aside, but James watched as she held the pistol out in front of her, with one hand holding the gun and one balancing Pete on her hip. She shot through the wall towards the group of men, injuring an outlaw on the other side. The wounded man dropped to his knees; being shot in the stomach he could only do so much, but he gave a desperate lunge through the door toward her. Marie, holding her brother, threw her now empty pistol at the attacker, jumped away from him and ran around her father's bed, to the other side of the room. She was losing strength and was also getting backed into a corner, and the outlaws knew it. She was trying to work her way to where she knew her father had stashed another pistol away. James could see through the door; his sister being backed into the corner and the evil faces of the men as they drew closer and closer to murder the rest of his dear family.

Tears streaming down his cheeks, anger and hate in his little heart; he cried as he beat his small fist against a piece of wood. "Please stop. Please stop." He loudly whispered, but none heard his pleading. The men with pistols drawn inched their way towards Marie. "Come on lass, we won't hurt ya." They mockingly laughed as they drew closer and closer to the frightened girl. Marie set Pete behind her father's nightstand and stood in front of it shielding the toddler. She glanced down at the place where she prayed the pistol would be. She saw it and quickly went for it. She dropped to her knees and pointed her gun up at the evil men, and fired into them, killing two more of the outlaws who underestimated her resolve and determination. But before she could get off another; they shot her. James screamed bloody murder, as they emptied their pistols, shot after shot, in rapid succession. He clutched his hands to his ears and cried, screaming for all his little body was worth, not caring if he could be heard, but the loud repeating gunfire made his little voice inaudible. Little Pete also was hit in the assault. James jumped at each shot with hands clinched and tears streaming down his face. He heard the brutal men as they started conversing among themselves.

"Ooww! - What a girl, she took down four of our men; not to mention this full-size bean-bag she shot in the gut. She was sure handy with a gun!" He heard one say.

"Who's to care? The house is ours, now what do we want?"

"Poor Dave. I knew him like a brother!" one man said looking down at one of his dead companions.

"Oh, shut up! You infamous cry-babe. I'm the one that ha'end to get shot!"

"Look for money, clothes, anything worth a dime. Humph!" one ordered.

As the men walked back into his observation room, James got a good look at each one of them. He couldn't help but look at them and their appearance; they all bore the image of horror and dread. One was dressed like a business man, a pocket watch hanging from his pocket, with a crafty and deceitful grin. One tall man had a long deep scar on his left cheek; and his eyes were as deep and mean as his scar.

One was a Mexican warrior with a small earing in his right ear. The last who wobbled out, was a short stubby man who carried two pistols and he had a long mustache, but what James noticed about him was he

was the one Marie had wounded; blood caked his shirt.

James' eyes were bloodshot with tears, he watched in horror as they tore apart his home. They looted his father's library and his desk, cursing and swearing as they went. They plundered his mother's china, and found his father's money stash, hidden behind a loose stone in the fireplace mantle. The kitchen was ransacked; and the bedrooms were pillaged.

Then another movement caught James' eye, he jerked his head towards the door, and to James' bewilderment a man that he had not seen yet, stepped into the open doorway, rain dripping from the brim of his hat. He was tall, his brown cowboy hat was tied under his chin, and he was dressed in the garb of a rich bandito. He had a tan vest of mountain lion skin, and a half poncho over his neck and shoulders. Horror and disbelief etched his face as he gazed upon the wreckage that had once been James' peaceful home. He glanced around the room, and then looking down at his feet, jumped back when he saw James' father lying on the ground.

"What in the name of almighty God?" he muttered as he quickly bent down. He felt his pulse to see if there was any hope. Then he looked into the bedroom and saw the whole scene of the last event that had drained everything out of little James' soul.

"Wha-What in God's name have you done?" He addressed his company. "Who do you think you are to come into this family's home and murder everyone? The man's gun is still in his holster, you cowards. Would to God I can just leave this whole operation! You have disgraced our revolution against the Mexican government, t-to now just a pack of relentless murderous outlaws. I said to come down here and demand food, yes; because we are desperate, but this is not what I meant. Now leave!"

"Ha! I sense weakness in the 'General'. Does the sight of a little blood and death, cause you to curl up inside? I say, done with you, Brock. You have been growing weak these past weeks. Starting now I am in charge. You need to have guts to be a leader; and I have plenty of that. Men, take him out and get rid of him!" Demanded Frederik, the one who bore the appearance of a business man.

Calmly, with his thumbs hanging on his gun-belt, Brock walked up to Frederik. "Weak, Frederik? Well I'm a gonna tell you somethin!" Brock jumped and grabbed Frederik by the lapels of his suit. "This was your last trip with us! And we can walk right outside and settle this if you like...civilly." He paused, then pushed Frederik away. "Willie, take him out and put him on his horse, and you better ride hard, fast, and far, Frederik. Leonardo, Travis burn this house down. And hurry, in a few days the whole 'nited States Cavalry will be upon us after what ya'll 'ave done!"

With more respect for Brock, the men listened to him. Frederik was ushered out and the men busily started dripping lamp oil all over inside the house.

"Light it, Leonardo!" Brock commanded as they backed out of the door. The empty oil container was thrown through the doorway where it rolled across the floor and came to a rest against father's booted foot.

Leonardo tossed the match igniting the lamp oil. He then turned and mounted his horse, riding off with the other outlaws.

Brock stopped, taking one last look back into the house, that was beginning to go ablaze, and reviewed the despicable scene. He saw his men, dead laying before the teenage girl. He turned away, his rage inside knew no limits. He, although being a rough mountain man, and hardly cared for the living or the dead, still had a modicum of moral restraint and was incensed at his men's show of cruelty. As Brock turned to go, he caught the glimpse of movement beyond the flames, that with every moment were rising higher and higher. Coughing and sputtering, a small boy was frantically climbing over a pile of wood. He stopped and suddenly, their eyes locked onto each other.

In an instant, Brock sprang back into the burning house to where James had been hiding. James got up to run, but before he could go anywhere, Brock caught him. In the confusion, James was grabbing for anything and he reached out and grabbed Brock's necklace, the pendant of the necklace was the shape of a silver skull. Brock turned to flee through the front door, but the flames had engulfed the exit. Surveying the room, Brock dashed passed the kitchen and kicked open the back door, escaping into the rain drenched night.

"Stop-Stop your struggle!" James kicked and punched and struggled, but to no avail. He went limp and fainted in Brock's arms.

In June of 1884, Burlington, Wyoming was a pretty quiet town; but was so situated that every now and then bands of outlaws passed through with nefarious intentions. Outside the town a few miles, there was a cave hideout for a group that called themselves "Los Forajidos" or "The Outlaws." The fear of them spread throughout those mountains; for they always looted and robbed when least expected; no local law had been able to stop them.

There was a certain young man that lived down a backroad outside the town, his dwelling was a simple, small log house. The house was built next to an old barn, on a grassy knoll, facing a nice average sized pond. The house was cheaply and quickly put together, and every eye that saw it could tell it was built in a sad and sorrowful way. The view outside his kitchen window showed three small white crosses which marked three graves; and a big black pile, a pile that always brought grim memories every time it was gazed upon. Burnt and charred boards rose from the large pile, and a blackened chimney stood like a scorched memorial of pain on the back side of that great heap.

On the small table was a Henry Rifle and some shells. Next to the rifle, an old Bible laid open; it had been burnt, and what was left of it was open to a very familiar and special psalm; and although mostly unreadable, it always spoke volumes every time it was looked upon. On the wall above the fireplace, hung a set of mule deer antlers; and on the floor next to the fireplace, a mountain lion head and skin.

Outside gunshots were fired; one, then two, and then in rapid succession - then all was quiet. Behind the house, a nineteen-year-old young man, was shooting a six-shooter. He was dressed in a tan cowhide jacket, black pants and boots, a dark brown cowboy hat and a black gun-belt. He was drawing and shooting at a fast rate of speed. He was learning the trade, for he was embarking on a mission that required this skill. He holstered his gun, walked to a rail and set old glass bottles on it; then he walked back to about fifteen feet away. Then aiming for the bottles, he would feather the hammer in fast sequence, every shot hitting its mark, then he would drop and roll standing up quickly then firing, then he would carefully take his aim, and at ten paces take the head off a nail. He was known in the town, as 'Fast James,' his name was, James Cassidy.

A rider came up from behind him. "Hey James...heard you shooting. How you farin'?"

"Oh, hey Sheriff Brown. I'm thinking everything's fine. Coming to check on me, huh?" James filled his pistol with new rounds.

"Nooo, no...just came out to tell, or remind you that our church is having a get together Sunday evening and you're welcome to come. You know, the town's yearly get together." The Sheriff informed him, unbuttoning his vest.

"Yeah Sheriff, I'll definitely be there. Thanks for the invite!" replied James, looking down the bore of his Colt Peacemaker 45.cal. He twirled the pistol on his trigger finger a few times, as he holstered his Colt.

"Son, don't forget you're always welcome at our home." The Sheriff looked out of the corner of his eye, to the burnt pile and the graves. He grimaced at the memory of his coming and finding James curled up in a hay wagon, fainted. He never knew what really happened to his friend and family.

"Thanks, Sheriff. Sometimes I might gonna need that. But I do belong here, this is where my family is. I do thank ya for raising me these gon' ten years and caring for me. And I love ya'll, as I would love my own family." James turned and started to walk away.

"James!" James stopped and turned his head slightly to listen to his godfather. The Sheriff pulled on the reins of his horse to stop the sudden jerk his grey stallion had made. "God will make all things right. He promised!"

The Sheriff waved with his hand and rode off. James thought about those words, "God will make all things right. He promised!" Is God really going to? The terror of that night's scene he saw as a child, continuously invaded his mind. He would inevitably recall scenes of that dark night, etched deeply into the private and painful recesses of his soul; the last look in his sisters' face, love and goodbye written in her blue eyes, his father lying there in a pool of his own blood, a vivid recollection of the murderer's ungodly faces as they plundered and ransacked their home.

Even as he stood there with his hand on his gun, and the other shielding his eyes that had begun to run, he grimaced inside at the remembrance. He swore in that day that he would take vengeance on them that in cold, innocent blood murdered his family. But how would he do this? Could he do this? Is it God's will for him to kill the men who murdered his family? Would his trying to find the men and kill them for murder be justice, or just a way to vent his anger? He read his bible day in and day out and found that many times vengeance was sought out and delivered. He clung to the concepts of God's justice which he saw in the "kinsman redeemer" and the "avenger of blood." But could he apply that to his life and circumstance?

As he thought on these things, leaning against a big wide oak tree, a man on a tan horse slowly rode up. James quickly jumped behind the tree he was leaning against. The man was clothed in buckskin, a long knife hung from one side, and a pistol on the right. He had curly, black hair, and his appearance looked like he was sad and had a heavy burden. The man did not see James; but went straight to the three graves and dismounted. James couldn't believe what he was seeing, a stranger was interested in his families' graves. James tightened his gun-belt and quietly, taking advantage of the man's reverie, walked up close behind the man.

"Stranger?"

In that split second, the man spun around and had a gun in his hand. James gave the man an uppercut punch to the jaw, grabbed his arm, and banged it against his own leg, knocking the weapon from his hand. Grabbing him by the lapels, James threw him against his horse. James stared into the thin tanned face with a small beard. A hint of recognition called as though from a great distance, the face intruding on the misty edge of memory, but he couldn't be sure. For a fleeting moment, his flaring nostrils perceived the indistinct electrical charge of a thunderstorm, then it was gone like the fading memory of a distant flame.

"Hey...now just'a, wait a minute boy." He paused, rubbing his cheek. "Nobody just does that without me a'fightin' 'em afterwards. But I was the one in the fault. You scared me, Lad!"

"What do you want here, Stranger?" James asked now on edge with this eerily familiar face.

"I saw what happened here ten years ago," the stranger batted his hat against his hand, knocking the roads dust from the top. "I saw how these good people were murdered. I couldn't believe what was goin' on, I burst in and tried to help but I was too late. I have felt guilty for all these years, after this happened; just the memory of this invaded my dreams. So, I decided to come see this place and beg for these poor soul's forgiveness."

"Did you know them?" James asked, not sure if this man was telling the truth or what his intentions were.

"No...I did not! Never met them, never had the opportunity." The man replied, combing his hair back with his fingers.

"So where have you been for these ten years? Why did you pick now to make your peace?" James folded his arms over his chest.

The man looked at the ground and picked up his pistol in the dirt and holstered it. He stood and looked at James. "I have been in prison, on a false charge. It was just a couple of days ago I was released." The stranger got back onto his horse.

"Ooh, I see. Well, I'm glad your soul is at rest now." James said, tipping his hat, contemptuously.

"Aye, it is...but now I'm after those men, to kill e'm for what dey done!!"

"Sir, do you know the men?" James asked, this man now had his full attention.

"Yes, I do...Personally!" The man spit out the response. He had so much hate in his voice, that it even shook James.

"What would be your name?"

"Brock...Brock Gilmore."

"Well Brock, I have to tell you something. That's my family buried there. It was my father, sister, and little brother that died that night. I watched it happen as well. So, if anybody goes after them, it's gonna be me. And it is my God blessed duty to kill those murderers and bring them to justice." James announced, resolution in his voice.

James watched in bafflement at the face that came over Brock. When he said that it was his family that had died that night, his face dropped from revenge and hate to distress and pain, it was almost as though James had stabbed him in the stomach with a knife. Brock just dug in his heels and sped off; leaving James in total confusion.

"Hey you, come back! I kinda, sort'a wasn't through!" James yelled for him to stop, but he kept on riding. "Interesting." James muttered.

Later that evening, James rode into town and went to Aunt Judith's Café; he loved to eat dinner there on Saturdays. It was a small and basic place to relax and they had good things to eat. As he was eating, in his favorite spot by the window, looking out into the street, he saw Brock Gilmore go up to the Sheriff's office door and knock, but nobody answered. James stood up and walked to the cafeteria door.

"Brock Gilmore!" James called out to the stranger that had paid him a visit at his place earlier. Brock turned and looked toward the café to see who was calling, for all he knew he was a stranger in this town. James just gestured with his arms for him to start walking; Brock came with a hop.

"Oh... It's you!" Brock said as he approached.

"Oh come on, you still got a grudge over me for sluggin' your chin?"

"Huh! That's the least of my problems boy!" Brock announced rubbing his chin.

"I just wanted to meet you proper like and invite you to eat dinner with me." James invited.

"Well, I think I'll take you up on that offer. I need me some home fresh food in my gullet."

They walked in and James motioned to the waitress to bring another meal.

"Well James tell me bout yourself?" Brock asked as they sat down.

"Well what exactly?"

"Just anything!"

"Okay...I'm nineteen, I am the son of Reuben Cassidy. He died as you know...or let me rephrase that, he was murdered. I am now on a chase for the five wicked, evil murderers that murdered my family. That's my life!"

"What skills would you happen to know?"

"Skills? That is such a broad..."

"I mean skills enough to chase five men, who are cunning, who are themselves skilled, and who are wicked. James, you may have a just cause, but you don't wanna get yourself killed." Brock instructed, he nodded to the waitress as she brought him his food.

"Well, I'm the fastest gun in the state!" James had a spark of hope.

"But, James, unlike your opponents, you have character. While you would never shoot somebody in the back, they would do it without even thinkin' about it!"

"Yeah, I see what you mean. What all do you know?"

"Well, I was a trail scout in the Civil War, then in '68 I was an Indian scout for General Custer, so I know a little bit. Yes, I remember it; I was leading the artillery wagons when Custer had his last stand. I saved our band of fifty cavalry; we were totally surrounded. Aye, I remember it as if it were yesterday. We were stuck in a valley, in between two mountains coming out of a draw, surrounded and engulfed in a deep forest. We heard them coming slowly and had just watched Custer and his six hundred men fall like wheat before its shearers. There was no way for us to escape. But we still could deceive the savages, cause we were in a dense wood. We had twelve cannons in our train; I ordered them all lined up in a circle but a wide circle, and to fire and not stop firing. Aye, and I ran through the Indian line and killed my share of Indians and passed them about a mile to a corral of our horses, around forty, I'd say. Then I tied them in a line and galloped back towards the Indians. Within four hundred yards they retreated and ran every which way, thinking more horse soldiers were on the way. Hahaha! Even though we lost the fight, I won a great victory in rescuing forty men from the savages."

"I see, I'll might wanna get some pointers along the way."

"And I'll be glad to help you anyway I can, these men are the ones that put me behind bars, I hold a grudge with 'em too, but I'm sure not as near big as what you have over them."

So, after they had eaten, they shook hands and left the cafeteria.

,,,

The next morning was Sunday. The little Burlington church was full, since in the evening there was going to be the annual town get together. The pastor preached about how God's love and judgment were the same and equal.

"In the teachings of Jesus Christ, the element of judgment is always brought out — it is the sign of the love of God."

James listened as the preacher spoke.

"For God hates sin, but at the same time loves mankind as a whole. Not wishing that any man perishes, but that all comes to repentance. But God's love for man does not supersede his justice. For justice to be done, judgment must come upon those who violate His law of love." James' back straightened, leaned forward slightly, deftly absorbing the preacher's words. "Through the recompense of God's wrath on evil doers, He expresses his love for the rest of His creation. Without wrath against the lawless, there is no love for the lawful."

After the preacher had finished his message, they sung a hymn. As church was dismissed, James looked over and noticed that neither Sheriff Brown, nor his daughter were there; which was very uncommon, so uncommon in fact, that it disturbed James. Pulling his hat off the hook and slipping it on, he shook the pastors' hand and thanked him for his sermon, then walked down the church steps, and headed toward the Sheriff's office.

The door hung slightly ajar. He pushed it open with the edge of his left hand, resting his right on the butt of his gun. "Hello, anybody here?" James asked, stepping inside. Something was wrong – he could sense it.

The door slammed behind him.

"Now how 'bout you just drop the gun-belt, seein's I got a pistol pointing to'ards your back!" A voice from behind him whispered. James thought he knew the voice, it sounded very familiar.

"Oh, of course...yeah, drop...belt." James reached for his buckle to take it off.

"HAHAHAHA! I got you back!! It's me...Brock Gilmore. That was really a good'n!" Brock slapped his back laughing away. Brock was proud of himself for he thought that he got James back for punching him, it was then he noticed James wasn't laughing.

"The Sheriff?" James asked, not even laughing at the intended joke; buckling his gun-belt back tight.

"I ain't gotta foggiest, I came down to talk to him about some business, and he wasn't here; wasn't here yesterday either." Brock glanced around the little room.

"The weirdest thing is he wasn't at church; he's always at church. Sick or well, dead or alive!"

"Well what'cha got in mind, Lad?"

"I'm gonna head over to his house and check there; maybe Dorothy, if she's there, will know something."

"Dorothy?" Brock asked.

"Uh yeah..." He cleared his throat with a hint of condescension.   "His -uh- cat." James answered mockingly.

"A cat...named Dorothy?" Brock asked in bewilderment, an eyebrow protruding upwards; sometimes Brock acted like a totally senseless individual, with the little he knew of him.

"It's his daughter, Imbecile." James rolled his eyes; this guy was probably the worlds true nincompoop.

"Ooh ok...figures." Brock looked at the young man who he had saved ten years ago with admiration. He wasn't going to tell him yet about the truth, of what happened on the night that haunted both their memories, because he knew that every time the subject was brought up James' face would ignite in determined anger and ferocious revenge. So, he kept this a secret, but he knew one day inevitably James would find out the truth that he was the Brock of that terrible night.

James ran over to the Sheriffs house which wasn't far. He opened the little white picket fence that lead to the house and bounded up the steps. Looking in the reflection of the door, he desperately tried to fix his hair with his fingers, he tucked in his black shirt, and knocked. Dorothy opened the door and greeted James.

"Hey James, sorry I couldn't make it to church. I was really busy getting stuff prepared for tonight." She started to make conversation, not realizing James needed to talk, she jokingly added. "We're gonna have a lot of goodies."

"Oh of course, yeah that's fine...I-I'm sure you were busy, where's your Dad?"

"He wasn't at church?" She asked in worried dismay, although she didn't know exactly what to be worried about. "He said he was going to church, and that he would be out all day and he'd see me tonight. Do you think something is wrong?"

"Well, all I know is that your dad would have to be stuck or deceased to miss a church service." James replied, fingering his hats brim in his hands.

"Yes, I know...well let me know as soon as you know something."

"Alright, that I will." He fitted his hat back on as he made his way for the door.

James walked out of the house, down the steps, and over the walk, deep in thought on another planet.

"Any important information?" Brock chuckled as he spoke.

Startled, James spun around and there laid Brock, leaning against a tree. He had his hat pulled over his eyes, and a straw hanging out of his mouth. His hands folded behind his head, a giant and mocking grin spread over his face.

"Aaaah! You idiot! One day you're gonna get yourself shot spookin' me like that, and I ain't kiddin'." James yelled at Brock.

"James did something happen? I heard you yell!" Dorothy came out of the house and asked. Brock rolled in laughter, James turned and glared at Brock.

"Umm-yeah...uh, uh, a buzzard flew up into the tree I scared it off, it-it it's gone, it shouldn't come back, but then again it might. Ahem." James desperate for an answer, was snapping his fingers, searching for a quick reply.

"Oh--Ok," She put her finger to her lips. "I don't think I have ever seen a vulture in that tree." She snickered and strolled back into the house. She had seen the whole thing, for she had gone to the window to see James ride away.

"What's the idea in callins' me a buzzard?" Brock questioned, pulling the straw out of his mouth for a moment.

"Chiefly, because you have the wee-yon pea-sized brain of said buzzard! Forget it, we gotta find the Sheriff!" He scolded in no more than a whisper, as Brock shrugged his shoulders, and threw the straw back into his mouth.

James and Brock rode down the street, and back toward the Sheriff's office again, to see if there would be any evidence to where he could be. They opened the door and walked in. The desk was full of many 'wanted' posters, James fingered through them thinking he would find out, if maybe the Sheriff went out chasing some outlaw, which was very unlikely for Sunday morning but possible.

As he carelessly thumbed through the posters, the pile that he had always seen laying on the Sheriffs desk every time he walked in. He then came across one picture that shook him like a thunderbolt. He slowly and painfully picked it up, his eyes crossed, and the figure on the poster faded into a blur, and his head ached from a memory. Brock seeing James furious face, walked over to where he was standing and looked at the poster. It was a Mexican man who had a large charro hat, a cunning and cruel face, and in his right ear a small earing. James recognized him as the Mexican warrior of the raid on his home, ten years before. James, small beads of sweat dripping down his face, closed his eyes as he clenched his fist, crumpling the poster in his hands. Brock saw James face and turned away. James dropped the poster carelessly to the floor and leaned over on the desk.

"Brock, you said you know the men who murdered my family?" James asked as he stared down at the left corner of the desk.

"Yes, I knew 'em James." Brock picked up an item off the floor.

"Is this one of the men?" He picked up the poster revealing its details to Brock.

"It is...his name is Leonardo Raphael, he calls himself, 'Diablo Encarnado'. And be careful friend he lives out his nickname."

After a moment of silence, "Where is he?" James asked tilting his head towards Brock behind him.

"James, I'll tell you after we find the Sheriff."

"I gotta know!" James almost in tears, spun around grabbing Brock by the collar, shook him and yelled in his face. This was his first objective and this stranger Brock was not going to stand in his way.

"James, Sheriff Brown could be in danger. When you were lookin' at the poster, I found this stuck in the floor by the cell door." Brock held up a long knife.

James forgetting about the poster for the moment, knew something was wrong. They ran out to the front of the Sheriff's office and examined around the horse rail, they saw that about three horses had come that morning and four had left. They jumped on their horses and galloped out of town, following the fading tracks, and leaving a cloud of dust. Dorothy watched out of her window as the two riders left the town, scrubbing a bowl she had used to mix her baked goods in.

With Brock leading, they followed the tracks to a mountain top outside the town, they stopped and examined the valley below. A beautiful big green forest lay below, with the glorious blue Greybull River twisting through the green woods. The sunset lowering cast an orange glaze on the long, snaky river. Brock looked over at James, "You see what I see?"

"Scenery! What do you see?" James answered a little in mockery; for he was not fully there, for half of him was still leaning over looking at the poster, down at the Sheriff's office.

"Scenery!" Brock repeated James answer, definitely irritated. "My friend James, I say it again, if you are going to be on the look for five men who murdered your family, then you are going to need to learn how to track 'em. They are cunning, worse than animals!" He situated in his saddle, his leather saddle creaking as he moved. He pointed beyond him. "I seen two campfires. See them small wisps of smoke comin' up over that big rock pokin' out of the mountain about a mile or so, south of the forest?"

"You bet, I do. Shall we try there?" James answered a little relieved that they had made some progress.

"Let's go!" They dug in their heels and sped away.

Within a couple hundred feet of the camp, they quietly got off their horses, and slowly walked closer and closer, ever so ready for action. They squeezed into the mountain crevice above the campfires to see what they were going to be dealing with. They reached a rock boulder and leaned over.

"Well, what do we do first, pal?" James asked breathing hard after walking a few hundred feet.

"James, first things first, we're going to have to get rid of this Mexican dog behind us!" Brock whirled around and threw his knife. A tall man with a rifle and bandolier strap, was coming at them with his long war knife. But as Brock's knife found its mark, the scout dropped dead at their feet, without a sound. James stared at the dead outlaw, he couldn't believe that he didn't hear the scout coming up behind him. "You have to sharpen your senses, young friend! To live in this wilderness, especially on the mission you have begun, you must grow eyes on the back of your head. Come on." He roughly slapped the back of James head, James quickly and with hardly another thought, situated his hat back straight and continued.

They creeped down the mountain, their boots making dangerously loud clops on the rocks. They kept a lookout for other scouts; James, trying to be a little more cautious than before. Down in the valley, they saw a figure sitting next to a tree, was it him? It was so far away they couldn't really tell from the distance.

"Is that the Sheriff down there? He sure ain't makin' any racket." Brock asked smelling the barrel of his pistol.

"It looks like him." All of a sudden, the man tied to the tree yelled. "At least you can't say I didn't warn you when I part your hair with my pistol, cold as death!"

"Ahem. It's him!" James coolly and collectively affirmed.

Two guards paced back and forth in front of him. He was sitting there trying to pull at the ropes that bound him. Brock and James looked at each other, they knew that treachery was afoot.

"Alright James," Brock pointed down below, and began to explain to James what they had to do. "There's three scouts that we're going to have to take out, before we can get down there."

"Where?"

"Ahem! Look, over there sitting on that stump, then there, and then over by that horse fence. I'll take the two on the wood line, you take the one at the horse fence. Do not shoot, less'n you gotta! Throw your knife! I count only six guys down below, that ain't the whole group, there's supposed to be more, a great deal more, I think that there could be danger afoot. Be careful!" Brock gave his orders, then was lost in the woods.

James started heading over to the scout, quietly, cautiously he stepped closer to his first objective. His heart raced, but his mind alert. All of a sudden, he was jumped by something from up in the tree, he crumpled to the ground at the sudden weight that hit him from above; whatever had fallen onto him fought with vigor and strength. Whoever it was, was of equal strength to James. They wrestled for a time, then finally James found his opening and pulled back and punched his attacker with his favorite uppercut to the jaw. The man flew back and landed against a tree; and laid there. James stood there his gun-belt twisted around him, and his shirt, now untucked; he rubbed his mouth with his sleeve and it was then when he noticed, it was an Indian. He walked closer to try to help him up. Then the Indian jerked James to the ground and jumped on top of him, bringing his knife dangerously close to James chest; black braids fell into his face. Holding the Indians' knife away from him, he wrested it from his hand, punched him in the stomach, and threw him off of himself.

"Injun. Stop!" James now put him in a lock position, that he was not going to get out of.

"You one of them?" The Indian asked in a measured tone and pointed to the outlaw stronghold.

"No, I've come to save a friend." James tried to convince him as he released his grip. This 'Injun' speaks English.

"Then maybe I can help you, and you can help me." The Indian stated presumptuously.

James startled at this sudden proposal, laughed. "Ahem! Well, seein's that we had such a nice and warm friendly-like greeting, I figure that we are as good as comrades. I warn you though, this six shooter, that hangs on my side never misses its mark. So, don't try anything. Now we gotta get rid of that scout by the horse corral, then we open fire on the camp and release that man sitting next to the tree. Did you get all that, or do I have to do all the hand signs and such?" James noticed that the Indian did not look confused.

"Oh I got it...I hate these outlaw savages."

"Why?" James asked fixing himself back up from his scuffle with the Indian.

"Revenge! I am needing to settle an issue with these banditos." The Indian wiped the dirt from the blade of his knife, where he had swung and missed James.

"Vengeance, revenge, that seems to be everybody's aim and goal these days." James said abruptly.

"It's too bad that there is so many evil people in this world." The Indian had big eyes as he spoke.

James marveled at the logical reason that came from a savage, in his heart he hoped he would come to know this Indian. The two crept closer and closer to the scout, who at that time had took the opportunity to grab a snooze. James threw his knife, and it found his mark. The scout jumped up grabbing for his back then toppled over dead; James and his new friend, waited for Brock's signal.

Minutes later, Brock gave his signal, and he started firing; he shot three men immediately. James, Brock and the Indian, quickly took over the unfortified fort. James ran over to the Sheriff, and while he was untying him, he asked. "Why'd they do this?"

"We don't have much time to waste. We need to ride hard and fast. They're going to raid the town get together in a couple hours, I don't know what their purpose is, but they took me hoping that without a sheriff the people would offer less resistance."

"What?"

"Friend, we got to get to town before those 'Forajidos' do, or the town of Burlington will be no more." The Indian picked up a rifle, from one of the dead men.

"Thanks, but you don't need to-"

"We go, now." The Indian mounted a horse and headed off. James, Brock, and the Sheriff ran toward their horses and galloped away.

"Now where'd an Indian like that come from?" Brock asked as they rode.

James sat and thought for a moment, then announced. "Heaven. He came from the high blue yonder!" James smiled to himself; he knew the Lord had sent this Indian to be a friend and comrade in his work. Brock stared at James with his usual one high eyebrow.

They rode to the end of the wood line, and out in the distance. Over the meadow, they saw a group of about thirty outlaws heading toward the town, slowly taking their time, waiting for nightfall.

"Man, if they were allowed to just walk in, they would take the town on accident!" Sheriff Brown muttered.

"Well, we're gonna give them a warmer reception then they had planned." James pulling on the reins, spun around on his horse and looked up.

In the distance on the mountain top, in the evening sunset, he saw an Indian brave galloping at full speed toward Burlington. "Now that is a picture!"

"That's the same Indian?" Brock asked.

"Aye, it is!"

The sun finally faded away, and night had fallen in Burlington. Riding at a full gallop the whole way allowed them to reach the town before the outlaws. Soon they came into the town, and there was music and food, children played four-square in the middle of the street, men and women all around enjoyed the evening, everybody was having a grand time. But as they rode in, the party ceased, everybody saw the three cowboy riders, and knew something was wrong. Dorothy came running up to her father.

"Pa, what happened? What's wrong?"

"I'm fine, sweetheart." He put his arm around her. "But friends," He addressed the crowd. "I want every man to put on his gun and be next to a rifle; be ready to defend your wife and family. The 'Los Forajidos' are coming!"

The crowd started to panic. "We've stationed twelve men of our militia on each side of the town. The outlaws have to get to them before they get to us. But we have to act like nothing is wrong, so they don't suspect anything. We've got about half an hour. Come on, play fiddlers! This is a night of celebration!" He tried to cheer the crowd as the frightened musicians started playing again.

Brock and James positioned themselves behind the militia and in front of the crowd, on a rooftop. They waited for the outlaws to approach, James watched in the direction he saw them positioned last. He looked at where the last glow of the sun was visible, hoping that maybe his peripheral would catch movement in the formidable darkness. Straining his eyes into the indefinite blackness of night and shielding his ears from the noise of the fiddlers he desperately tried to locate where the heathen might be. Brock nudged James and pointed into the unknown blackness, James looked and there over the crest came a line of silhouettes. He shuddered for that moment's scene brought a memory of ten years past stampeding into the present; a memory of eight dark riders.

As the outlaws approached, they silently split into two groups; one took the south part of town, the other the north. The town militia was ready and started shooting. At the sudden burst of gunfire from the militia, many outlaws fell; but as soon as the first round from the militia was fired, the outlaws turned and charged. The militia held their ground, and after a few minutes of gunfire exchange, the outlaws retreated, and the gunfire ceased.

"What do you make of that?" James asked Brock, sweat dripping from his face. He had never been in a gun fight, and so his adrenaline was running high.

"I take it 'of that,' means the outlaws moving away?" Brock quickly refilled his pistol.

"Um, yeah kinda sort'a, what else?" James scornfully glared at Brock.

"My friend, you need to know that they are not retreating. They want you to think that. They're not withdrawing, they'll be back soon...one way or another."

"Gee thanks. Makes perfect sense!" James mockingly bowed to Brock.

A sudden cry came out, like that of a dying man. James instinctively and immediately jumped up and ran in full speed in the direction of where he heard the noise, he jumped and pulled himself up onto a roof and walked it to the other side; there he stopped. And there he saw the sight of an outlaw sheathing the knife he had used to stab one of the militia men. When he saw the outlaw kill the militia man, it put a burning rage in him that he never knew. James pulled out his own knife and jumped onto the man. The force of the blow made the outlaw drop to his knees, and James stabbed him through the shoulder. The murdering outlaw never knew what hit him, and never would. James turned around, and there stood two other outlaws with their knives. He spread his arms and prepared himself, never had he had another man on the other side of his gun for a duel. But he swiftly drew and shot them both before they could react. He reholstered his gun and jumped back up onto the roof. He alerted the crowd to be cautious because the outlaws had started to mingle and kill the militia. The militia was then called back into the middle of the town, and only seven showed up. They called them again but that was all that appeared.

Moments later, the outlaws on horseback, poured in from all sides. They had been hurt very bad for they only had a total of ten men, the others had been killed. Their leader led the way and halted them in front of the frightened crowd. He lifted his leather gloved hand and slowed to a stop.

"So, I see that you were informed we were coming. I have learned that secrets have as much a chance of staying secure, as it does for water to stay in a bottle with a hole in the bottom. Now we have come for the town bank, my spies informed me that a shipment of twenty-thousand dollars went into this bank last night; we want that, and demand nothing more, now let us in or we will finish to the full extent what we can do!"

James looked at the crowd, for the bank to be robbed would mean the town would suffer terribly. He looked at the Sheriff who had his arm around his daughter. The frightened crowd talked back and forth to each other. And the distraught look on the banker's face was enough to settle in his mind the certain truth; his town was in trouble. Brock glanced over at James, wondering if he recognized the leader of the group yet, he knew that his young friend might get himself killed in a few minutes if he would identify the gloved rider.

James looked back towards the outlaws, he jumped off the roof he had used as a shooting position and walked toward the leader. The Sheriff called out to him, Brock tried to stop him; but James didn't hear any of it. He hid behind a pillar and refilled his pistol with new bullets. He then walked to the leaders' horse, and it was then and only then, when he realized the leader was the man in the poster, Leonardo Raphael.

In that split second, an invasion of new memories of that horrible night with his family came into his mind. His head whirled, his back began to ache, a dizziness of body and soul came over him, and his vision blurred; this was one of the five that was there on that dreadful night. He began to burn inside, revenge and godly hatred boiled in his veins. He looked deeper into the eyes of this wicked man. In only a minutes time, his mind replayed things that his childhood mind had forgotten of the incident. He stepped a few steps back, his boots making definite imprints in the earth. And in a shaky, but yet bold voice, he demanded for Leonardo to unmount his horse. Leonardo did, thinking that whatever this kid wanted, could easily be taken care of in a matter of seconds. But he was shocked when he heard James speak...

"Leonardo Raphael, Son of the Devil, as you claim that name as your title. I be standin' fifteen feet in front of you on this night. And I stand here in God's name to avenge the death of my father, my sister, and my little brother that you and a few others came in and ruthlessly murdered. Murdered, in cold blood! You forgot to get rid of a witness, and that witness was me! I watched the whole entire scene, and now for the honor of my family, and of my duty to God, I am here to bring your miserable and evil life to an end. At least I give you the opportunity to defend yourself. Draw your pistol, Diablo Encarnado, and defend yourself."

The crowd watching gasped in horror, for they knew the young man's wish to avenge his family, but they did not know he would actually follow through with his vow. Dorothy stood with her hand to her mouth, she knew only certain fate would happen in the next moment. The Sheriff called out again, but James stood like a solid, unshaken pillar in a storm.

Leonardo paused, bouncing from one foot to the other, with a nonchalant smirk on his evil face, roared with laughter, "Kid, I must warn you, I am not only a murderer and robber, but I can kill you on accident, with my high-speed draws. I am a gunslinger!" he patted his gun. "This gun has sixteen notches in the hammer, don't be added among them. I warn you! Your dead family ain't worth it."

James without a response, just glared at him. Seconds went by, as they stared at each other. Just then, a man behind Leonardo went to pull a gun on James; but a shot from above stopped him and killed him. The man dropped off his horse dead. James glanced over to see who just saved his life, and on the balcony of the church roof, stood an Indian proud and tall, he held up his Henry rifle, eagle feathers hanging from the barrel. A big smile spread across his face. Leonardo jumped at the shot, but James didn't even bat an eye.

In the next second, Leonardo spun and shot; but in that same second, James dropped prone on his stomach and in midair fired. As a by stander you would not have even noticed that two shots were fired, because they were both fired at once; two shots, but only James' counted. Leonardo jumped back, slamming against his horse, then went falling forwards, he was hit square in the chest and fell to his knees. He muttered in his dying breath, "Killed by a kid?" He dropped to the ground.

James slowly stood to his feet, his legs shaking, and adrenaline high, looked toward the outlaws that were left. "You vermin run and don't stop running till you cross the border back into Mexico." They turned and left, instantly, without a word.

Sheriff Brown, Dorothy, Brock, and a few others gathered around James. James walked over to the dead Leonardo and nudged the corpse with his feet. "Now you are in a place where you will forever be punished, Diablo Encarnado!" James looked back toward the church roof, he was still there. The proud and tall Indian, had a big smile across his face, and waved goodbye, disappearing into the night. James hoped he would see him again.

James turned to his friends. "Was tonight supposed to be a party?" They all laughed and turned back to the happiness of the night.

It was mid-June 1884, and the bright sun of summer shone strong and hot. That week, some few days after the shootout, James was hired on as a ranch hand on the big Whitmyre Ranch, about two miles south of the town. He loved the job; just him and his horse mending fence gave him time to think about his life. He was mending some fences one day, when he thought he heard a twig break behind him, as if someone was approaching. He immediately paused the twisting of barbed wire around the wood post he was mending. Tipping his hat lower, he turned slowly to see, glancing over his shoulder, but nothing was there. He walked slowly to where he heard the noise, but then from right behind him where he just came from, another noise. He started to go towards that noise when a louder and more definite noise came from the opposite direction. "Hmm. Must be snapping beetles!" Confused, James cautiously made his way to the latest noise. Then from out of nowhere he was jumped, the body that descended on top of him was heavy, he fell to the ground and turned quick with his hand on his gun, to see who this attacker was. It was the Indian he had met days before. The Indian stood above, pointing at him, and laughing for all he was worth. He stood laughing so hard, James had to chuckle to himself.

James leaned up onto his elbows, and with a smirk to himself, he let out a deep breath. "Soooo!" He paused, as the Indian continued to laugh. "Is that how you greet every person, every time you meet up wit' 'em?"

"Hahaha! I laugh at your ignorance." The Indian mocked as he stretched out his hand to help him up.

"My ignorance?" James gratefully gave him his hand.

"You looked very humorous down there chasing noises. That was me making all those noises."

"Uhm...yeah. I'm thinkin' I could a fig'rd dat 'ne out by now!" James replied, as he stood to his feet and brushed himself off.

"That's how Indians fool their prey or the enemies. They'd throw pinecones, sticks or anything heavy and throw it in the opposite direction, then their opponent will follow the noise - most of the time."

"So, was I your prey or enemy?" James asked not really giving a care.

"Well, I guess they could do it to their friends as well, although we have never met officially."

"I think we have met two times too many already, my name is James Cassidy." James said as he held out his hand.

"Aah! James Cassidy...I've heard of you, I am known as Hiawatha." They shook hands briefly.

"Would you be the one known as 'Fast James'?" Hiawatha asked inquisitively.

"The same, though I don't pride my life and existence on it but, it's there when I need it. By the way, thanks for saving my life a few nights ago. I was so furious in the moment, I totally forgot that people behind my opponent could've killed me."

"I was there to make sure everything stayed fair and even. But I was shocked at the speed of you with your pistol." Hiawatha sat down next to James, who had plopped down on the ground.

"I trained long and hard for that. But what I'm wondering right now is, how do you speak English so good? And you are never with a member from your tribe which is even more strange?"

Hiawatha took a deep breath, a long and deep sigh; and after a few minutes of getting his thoughts together he began. "That my friend is a simple, but yet hard question to answer. I know English because I went to an English school. I was banished from my tribe twelve years ago, when I was small. Two white men forced me to show them the place where to find, the gold on the lands of the Indian. My father had told me never to tell, and I never did. Until, these-these two white devil dogs came to me, they held a knife to my throat, telling me that I had better tell them where the gold was, or they would kill me. I tried to get free, I struggled and struggled, but then they tied me tight to a tree. I remember them as plain as I remember this

knife." He pulled a knife out of its sheath on his side, and holding the blade twirled it around and caught it by the handle. "You see this knife, this was their 'gift' that they gave me for betraying my people. I have only kept it at my side, to give it back to them, when the time comes, and I mean give it back to them, point first. The next day following was to be my birthday, and when I woke up and the drums that were supposed to be playing signaling my birthday were not, I knew why they weren't. I came out of the teepee, and my father was standing there. All he said was "Go far" and I walked away forever. I knew it wasn't my fault, it was either tell or die. I heard later, that two Indian braves were killed by whites looking for gold. I went into the mountains and searched for the men to kill them until I was lost in that great wilderness. By a year, I was skin and bone; I had not been eating properly. A white man found me brought me into his house and fed me. He sent me to school and I learned the ways of the white man. And then after I was old enough, I went on a quest to find the men that did that to me. And unlucky me has not found one yet."

"Why were you at the outlaws camp the night we met?" James asked as he remembered that evening.

"I heard through a source that the 'Diablo Encarnado' had a link to the man I'm after. I truly don't know where to find him. It's like a needle in a haystack."

"I know what you mean, Hiawatha. It is very hard to live with circumstances like that, I know. I have the same story but from another angle. One night while we ate dinner, a group of men just came in and killed my family when I was nine years old, right in   front of me. I sat there and watched my family murdered one by one. My older sister killed some of the attackers, but then after they did all they could do...they burned down our house."

44

"Huh. I would have loved to meet your sister; where were you when this happened? How did you manage to escape?" Hiawatha went onto his right elbow next to the tree.

"As I remember, I was in the wood-store, in the east side porch of the house."

"The house?" Hiawatha asked, starting a new wonder in James mind.

"The house?" For the first time James thought on this mystery. How could he possibly be in the house when it burned down?

Hiawatha pulled away from James and leaned back against the tree. "You're confused? Aren't you? My friend don't even think about it. I have learned that it doesn't help to think about bad memories long forgotten."

"No, I'm serious, how did I get out of the house?" James muttered forgetting even the presence of the Indian.

"Well I'm off about to roam through the woods, my daily pass time by the way. I'll probably see you soon."

"Alright...see ya later."

"James, thank you for being a friend. I've never had a friend before. In fact, I'd like to think of you as my brother."

"Me neither. You know I still wonder about that mystery that you brought up. Somebody had to save me and get me out. It does sound like we are on the same mission, Hiawatha, let's go together and each find these evil men."

"Among my people if you become close friends, then you become brothers. Can we become brothers for this cause that we have taken?"

"The good book says, can two walk together except they be agreed. It is not just a run of vengeance, it's a matter of Gods justice on earth. Sounds fine by me. Brothers we are!" James unhesitatingly answered Hiawatha without asking all that it entailed.

And then by the custom of his people, Hiawatha pulled out his knife and carefully cut his own wrist, then grabbed James arm and cautiously scored his wrist. Then they shook hands to where Hiawatha's cut met James' cut, and each other's blood flowed into the others. "We are now brothers." Hiawatha and James shook hands and started off on their new mission together.

5

Later that day, James rode up to the Whitmyre ranch house and tied his horse to the wooden rail. He had done his duties for the day and went towards the house to get his weekly pay. He climbed the steps and knocked on the door.

"Hello. Welcome James. How are you doing?" Mr. Whitmyre greeted him warmly.

"I'm doing well...the south fence is all back up and fixed. I believe that we are going to have problems with rustlers this year. I saw three cattle missing from the herd on the sixty acres."

"I was worried about that, I actually got-? What happened to your wrist?"

"Oh umm I-I, it got cut." James announced as he tried to brush it off.

"Got cut?" Mr. Whitmyre asked with one eyebrow up.

"Yess, got cut. I'm not sure about the rustlers...my brain actually isn't even in the mood to even think about it right now. Tomorrow I'll go out and look for horse tracks and see if I can tell where they're coming from."

"Alright that'll work. Here is your money, see you tomorrow." James left the ranch house and headed for town. He wanted to look at the wanted posters again and see if he could find one that would tell him who his next opponent would be. As he approached the town, he dropped his horse off at the stable, and walked into the post office to see if he had any mail. He gathered his mail and walked back out.

As he strode down the sidewalk looking down at his mail, he was met by Dorothy.

"Hey James." She walked up to him.

"Oh hey. How are you doing?" James asked tipping his hat, as he fingered through his mail.

"Fine. I'm running to the market to get some things for father's birthday tonight."

"Wow! With all the commotion of life I totally forgot it was his birthday today."

"Come tonight. I think it will do you good. The mayor and the deputy are going to be there too."

"I might." James said unassured.

"I'm so glad that you're alive." She announced abruptly.

"Ahem, why thank you, I am too." James sarcastically replied, dropping his unwanted mail in the post office trash barrel.

"Ha-ha! Nooo, I mean from the other night. As I stood there watching you in front of that wicked bandit. I was..." She paused, looking down at the ground. "I'm just glad that you are still alive. It scared me!" Dorothy stopped, and then finished.

"Yes, well I'll come; and I might bring a friend."

"A friend?"

"Yes...is something wrong with that?" James asked for it sounded as though she didn't approve.

"No...well I guess not." They said goodbye and James set out to find his friend.

He rode out of town and scanned the horizon; just then he caught a glimpse of smoke in the distance, little enough to be a small campfire. As he looked at the campfire smoke he thought a little high of himself for remembering to spot it, remembering Brock's words from the other night. His horse silently trotted toward the small camp, he tethered his horse to a branch, and slowly and silently walked toward the campfire. He pulled back some branches and peered out. An Indian spun a piece of meat on a stick, "Hahaha, here is my chance!" James schemingly muttered to himself, as he cautiously approached his friend. But right before he was going to jump onto his back.

"Hello brother James!" Hiawatha said his back still turned to James. James stopped in his tracks and immediately started coolly walking slowly up behind him.

"Ooh-fantastic...just great." James stated, putting his thumbs through his gun-belt, as if nothing had ever happened.

Hiawatha grinned to himself. "The way you came hopping in here, I suspect that somethin's got you joyful." James made a senseless face at Hiawatha's back for mocking him. He then came and sat across from Hiawatha.

"Ahem! Well, I came to ask you if you want to come with me to the Sheriffs birthday party." The smoke of the campfire slowly found its way around to him as he spoke, he got up and moved.

"Does he know you invited me?" Hiawatha put a piece of meat in his mouth.

"No, but he knows you saved me the other night; and that is enough." He coughed as he moved again, the smoke seeming to be after him; he stood up.

"Well then I'll go. Besides I had prayed that I could have a better supper for tonight and I started cooking this measly piece of meat, thinking my prayer wasn't answered; now look I go to a feast."

"Oh shucks, Hiawatha, come on."

The two mounted their horses and rode into town. A little later in the evening, they arrived at the house, where a few horses had already been tied to the rails, so they knew the party had started. They dismounted, and James made himself ready to walk into the party.

"You know, James I almost didn't come." Hiawatha glanced over the horse toward James as he spoke.

"Why's that?" James asked combing his fingers through his thick black hair.

"Have you ever felt like a fish out'ta water?" Hiawatha chuckled to himself, but he was still all the way serious.

"Ha! Don't worry I think they'll like you." James led the way into the party.

The party had started, and everybody looked up as the two young men entered. Dorothy was the first to greet them as they walked in.

"Is this your friend?" Dorothy asked in a little relief.

"Yes, this is Hiawatha. The one who saved my life the other night." James stated.

"Hello miss." Hiawatha raised his hand in his Indian style wave.

"English?" Dorothy asked, looking up at the tall Indian.

"No, I'm just talking anything, everything you might happen to understand." He joked, red as a beet, matching his native color.

"Humor?"

"Yeah he is pretty funny and uncertain!" James glinted up at Hiawatha; who was about a foot taller than him.

Then James looked over towards the Sheriff and saw Brock was sitting there talking to him.

"Brock, I thought you had left town. I hadn't seen ya." They both approached and shook hands.

"Oh no my boy...I've been hangin' around town waitin' on you." He lowered his voice as his sentence got longer.

"Waiting on me?" James put his finger to his chest, with his eyebrows up.

"Yeah, I wanna meet you somewhere tomorrow I've got something to tell you."

"Ok you wanna tell me tomorrow, not now?"

"Tomorrow!"

"Ok, just come out to my place, you obviously know where it is."

"Ookk. Be there around three o'clock."

"Okie-Dokie!" Brock turned and started talking with other visitors. "That was queer." James muttered to himself.

The Sheriff walked up and greeted them. The night was full of fun and entertainment. After the party, everyone slowly made their way home. James and Hiawatha were the last ones to leave; they talked to the Sheriff and Dorothy for a while, and then decided it was time for them to depart. They made their way to James house and slept there for the night.

In the morning, James awoke later than normal. He looked over to where Hiawatha had made a pallet on the floor; he was gone. James slowly walked to the window to see if his horse was still there. And there was Hiawatha, with a juicy piece of meat on a stick. James chuckled to himself. Later he came out of the house.

"Breakfast?" Hiawatha asked, holding up a stick with a hunk of meat on the end.

"Sounds good to me."

The two ate and then headed for town. On their way into town, James slipped through Whitmyre's "sixty acres", to see if he could find any clues of rustlers. Having Hiawatha with him he hoped he could help him find evidence of rustlers. They looked and looked but could not find any; so, by noon they gave up.

They had ridden farther than they had planned into the ranch. So, they rode into the nearby town adjoining the south-side of the big Whitmyre estate. Otto, Wyoming was a small town and it was a very quiet town.

As Hiawatha and James rode into the outskirts of the town, they looked down into the woods to their right, down in the valley. There below, was five men trying to hang a short little man; and the more the little man would fight to get away the more they would beat him. James, at once, reared his horse back onto its heels and sped away toward the appalling scene, his hat flying off; Hiawatha followed. As James approached, the hangers hit the horse, the startled horse went galloping away, and the man wobbled there, hanging. James pulled out his knife and cut the taut rope as he rode past. The hanging man dropped to the ground in a heap. James turned around and dismounted and ran up to the men.

"What is the idea in hanging a man like this? Where's the sheriff? Has he even seen a court of law?" James yelled at them, hair falling in his face.

"Who needs a trial when he's caught in the act?" One man yelled over the small tumult.

"You have just stopped us from showing justice." A tall man approached James, fingers in his gun-belt.

"Justice? Is justice hanging a man that hasn't had a trial? Where's even a sheriff? If this was a just case, a sheriff would be here!"

"He is a horse thief."

"Then bring him to the sheriff; and get it all done lawfully!"

Hiawatha bent down and unbound the man, but as he was getting up, a man behind Hiawatha hit him in the back of the head and knocked him unconscious. James punched the next guy closest to him and kicked the next intruder. But another was behind him and knocked him unconscious as well; the horse thief ran away in the confusion. The five men took them and locked them up in the sheriff's prison, under false charge.

It was still dark; but almost morning, before James came to and realized they were in prison. He slowly got up, his hand on the back of his throbbing head. He looked out the bars into the sheriff's office, and by a small candlelight, he could see a simple looking deputy laid back, legs on the desk, with his hat over his face, sleeping. He looked over at Hiawatha and felt the gaping wound in his head. "Boy, that idiot hit him hard." He tore part of his shirt and used it to bandage Hiawatha's head.

James sat there thinking to himself. He remembered that he was supposed to meet Brock at three the day before, he wondered what he could have possibly wanted. Then he imagined Brock sitting there waiting for him, pacing back and forth on his porch, then just walking in when the sun got too hot; the thought brought a smile to his face. But then his mind turned to thinking of sober things. His love for his family that was in heaven, and his God knew no limits. He wondered if chasing these murderers was inappropriate; he had already killed one and didn't feel bad about it. Then he thought about where the bandit was right then, and that brief thought made him shudder. After thinking a little bit more to himself, he pulled out his little bible, that he always carried in his tan jacket pocket, and walked to the casement to get some of the moonlight. He opened to the passage in the Old Testament, about the Israelites city of refuge, it was a place of shelter not for murderers; but for those who killed another man on accident. They were put there so innocent people could be safe from the avenger of blood. Murderers were not allowed in there, murderers were always brought to justice by death. He tried to figure out how that applied to his case. There was no city of refuge: prison was not a city of refuge, living a normal life ten years later was not a place of protection either.

As he deeply thought on these things, Hiawatha began to stir. James jumped over to him.

"You okay brother?"

"I'll live...I think! My head feels as though it has a cannonball sitting inside of it. And every time I even

move my eyes it bumps the side of my head and sends pain through my whole head system."

"Yyy-ea, well that could be bad, just stay layin' down calmly; it'll be morning soon enough." James shifted the prison covers around Hiawatha as he spoke, his own head still ached a little. He felt the lump on the back of his head.

The morning sun had just begun to peek through the bars, when the sheriff of Otto walked in, a cup of coffee in his hands. Yawning as he walked through the door, he glanced up and saw the deputy snoring. He rolled his eyes and yelled.

"JESSE! Wake up." He screamed to the top of his lungs. The deputy jumped pushing back on the desk, his seat flipped, and he fell out of his chair and went rolling out onto the floor.

"I-I, I'm awake, it's a lovely day, or rather, morning, isn't it?" He said, yawning, pulling up on the desk, big sleepy eyes peering over the table.

"HUH!" The sheriff rolled his eyes again.

"Ahem, Uhh...Sheriff." James called to the sheriff.

"Yeah, what do you want?" He yelled grabbing a sip of coffee.

"W-Why are we in here?" James asked innocently, scratching his head.

"Starting a fight...I'll let you out soon enough."

"Yeah, but...never mind."

James just sat back into his cot, why bother arguing, he decided. James sat back against the jail wall and rubbed his face with his hands.

Just then a short, stubby man entered the jail. James glanced at him as he walked in, the morning sun coming in with him. But the man's appearance shook James like a reed in the wind. With his hands still on his face, struck with the fierce wind of a remembrance, he slowly pulled himself up and walked to the bars. Where in the world did he see that man? But that man's face bore a memory in James mind that was not soon forgotten. Short, fat, stubby, two pistols, long mustache. His mind spun, when he realized that that was the man Marie had shot in the stomach on that horrible night that seared his heart and mind. He gripped the bars with all his might, drops of perspiration running down his face; he was one of the wicked murderers.

"Hiawatha, that fat guy...see 'im?" James tapped Hiawatha with one hand and pointed over to the short man with the other.

"Do I see him, hard to miss him. I also see your face...looks like you witnessed the devil and your long-lost ghost in an arm wrestle match, and you lost, and you have to live with it." Hiawatha said cutting his eyes down without moving his head.

"He was one of the men at the nights scene ten years ago." James whispered in measured beats, his eyes in a glossy stare, not blinking.

"No way. Ooww!" Hiawatha sat up fast, then moaned and grabbed his head from the searing pain that he felt through his head.

"I am absolutely certain." James stared at the stubby man, not even hearing Hiawatha's replies, as if he was in a conversation with no correspondent, his mind in another world.

"How can you be so positive?"

James turned his head towards Hiawatha. "When it comes time to kill him, there is going to be a piece of evidence that he was one of the murderer's, that he has carried with him to this day. That is the one that my sister plugged in the stomach."

"Oh-oh, I see what you mean!"

They silently sat back and watched the sheriff and the man talk. James paced back and forth impatiently waiting to get free and challenge the man. After the man left, the sheriff stood up and walked to the cell, fingering his keys.

"You guys have been so quiet, I'm curious, did ya'll do anything yesterday?" The sheriff fingered the keys as he waited for a response.

"Well we did get into a fight with five men. But-but that was after we stopped a hanging that they were trying to do. Then when we saved the man, they attacked us and knocked us senseless." James repeated what had happened and Hiawatha nodded slowly in agreement.

"I see. Yeah, I have been dealing with some people in this town who keep hanging people for horse stealing; its legal but I don't like it." He said as he opened the cell door. "Your free to go just don't get into any more trouble."

"Alright, Sheriff. We'll try...But just out of curiosity, who was that man that came in here a minute ago?" James asked.

"Willie? That was Willie Jeb, he owns the Mad Dog Saloon down the road a little bit." He described as he gave them their guns and weapons.

"Oh great!" James sighed.

"Why sounds like you don't like it that he owns a saloon!" The sheriff sat down in his chair after he pushed the deputy out.

"I swore I'd never go in a saloon, but this is different." James turned around and started to go out, tightening his gun-belt, then opening his chamber and looking to see if he still had his bullets.

"Um, excuse me intrudin' in your business like this...but it seems to me that somethin's goin' on I kinda need to know about." The look on Hiawatha's face gave it away to the sheriff.

"Why don't you come along? I'll need a witness." James opened the door and tipped his hat.

"Oh Lord, please no, my day just started?" The sheriff grabbed his shotgun and followed Hiawatha out the door.

James led the way to the saloon, Hiawatha and the sheriff followed. Hiawatha tried to explain to the sheriff as they walked. James stopped at the doors, and looked in. This was his first time to ever look into a saloon, and he sent a small prayer to heaven hoping it would be his last. He looked at the man behind the counter, he looked all around, but Willie wasn't there. He turned and looked back toward the sheriff and his Indian friend. Hiawatha waved at him signaling that he had his back, or did he, for with the other hand he was holding his aching head. James flung the small tavern doors open and entered; everyone turned around and looked at this young man, whose eyes showed fierce and rage. He stood and looked at each person seated down and at the bar.

"I've come to call on a man named, Willie Jeb."

"I'm Willie Jeb." Came a staticky, shrieky voice from the story above him. James looked up, and there he stood holding on to the railing and peering down below. James gazed into his eyes and he needed no proof to know that that was the man. He was wearing his two pistols and his long mustache gave him away. Willie came walking down the stairs and approached James. The look in James eyes spooked Willie a little. They stared at each other for a minute then all of a sudden James swung his fist and hit Willie in the jaw. He flung back and hit a pillar and shrank down. Willie answered his challenger, rubbing his jaw.

"Nobody boy, and I say nobody, hits me like that and lives to tell it!"

"Well you just might have to keep that little promise of yours." Replied James, looking down at the man on the floor, as he rubbed his own fist. The fat guy's head was harder than any other James had slugged.

Suddenly the building came alive; everyone that was in there jumped onto James. James stopped two men, another man threw a fist towards James. James grabbed his hand and twisted the attacker onto his back, kicking another man with his heel in the stomach. Another went to jump onto him, James caught him and threw him behind the bar. But then James had both his arms peeled behind him, and a man started repeatedly punching him in the stomach. James pulled himself up and kicked the man. He fought but then as soon as the rhythm of the beating to his stomach came again he couldn't pull up his feet and kick anymore.

Just when James thought he would go unconscious. BOOM! The sheriffs' shotgun blasted, plaster flakes fell from the ceiling.

"Now get up, you dumb rapscallions, come on get off him." The sheriff commanded. The sheriff got James and pulled him out of the saloon; James stood dizzy and hurting. He turned, and as he turned there stood Willie Jeb standing ten feet in front of him, still rubbing his chin. The whole wide-eyed crowd got quiet, knowing that whatever had started wasn't anywhere near finished. He slowly and painfully started walking to Willie, feeling his pistol making sure everything was in place. Willie stood there with a hand on each of his pistols.

"What's on your mind sonny boy?" Willie mockingly asked. James just continued to stagger towards him till he was about five feet away.

"You're right, killer. I do have something on my mind. Roughly ten years ago, on a little ranch outside Burlington. You know where I'm heading with this?"

Willie backed up a few steps, remembering that night. He knew right there, that there was going to be a shootout; but he did not reply.

"Ten years ago," he addressed the crowd of people standing there, keeping an eye on old Willie. "A group of men came riding to our house, I was only a child. But these wicked men came and murdered my family in cold blood. My father, my sister, and my little baby brother, then after that they burned our house to the ground. God knows why, I don't. I just saw the whole entire scene." He turned back to Willie. "Yeah that's right. I watched the whole thing transpire right before my childhood eyes. I remember when you attacked my sister and she gave you some heavy hot lead right through your stomach. Do you, admit to being there that night, Willie Jeb, or are we gonna have to show the sheriff...your stomach?"

Willie was shocked. He never thought he would have to deal with this in his life. The two stared at each other, eye to eye.

"Well youngster, you have brought me to the ring, let's just settle this like men." Willie chuckled as he pulled on his gun-belt to make sure it was in place.

"And my last words to you, I'm just gonna settle here on earth what will be officially settled in eternity." James declared biting his lip.

Enraged at these last remarks, Willie just drew and fired both pistols. But James was faster than Willie had thought; James fired and killed the murderer; but one of Willie's shots caught James in the upper shoulder. James his pistol flying, spun and grabbed his left shoulder, he stood there gritting his teeth from the sudden pain that inflicted his arm, he glanced over and looked at the dead Willie. His bullet had hit him in the neck, and thus did old Willie Jeb die in the streets of Otto, a town that he had once been the boss of.

Blood flowed fast from his shoulder and down his arm. He sluggishly walked over to the ghostly corpse; the stress of what just happened, and thoughts of his family drove him to tears.

With his left arm limp, he covered his eyes with his right hand and wept; the onlookers sadly looked away. Hiawatha, and the sheriff of Otto, started running towards him. The fatigue of his shoulder, and the extreme beating he had gotten before, had caught up with him. He swooned and fell beside the dead Willie.

"James!" Hiawatha ran up to James as he crumpled in the dirt, unconscious.

James and Hiawatha made their way to Burlington five days later; James wound had healed rather quickly. Remembering Brock's call to talk, James hurried to his house and found that Brock had made himself quite comfortable. He jumped off his horse and quietly crept into the house; Brock was snoring loudly on James bed. He crept up to the side of the bed and screamed.

"BROOOOCK!!!!"

Brock jumped up, as fast as a jackrabbit. He flew up so hard he bumped his head on the bed rail.

"OOOWWWW! You scalawag! What is the blasted problem with you for not showing up the other day? I waited all day for you." Brock held on to his aching head.

"And all night?" James asked laughing hard; Hiawatha had to walk outside he was laughing so hard.

"Yeah. Humph! What happened to your arm?" Brock didn't really think it was funny. Brock listened while James told him the events of the couple days before.

"So old Willie's gone." Brock drummed his fingers on the nightstand.

"Yep. And for good reason." Hiawatha replied leaning his chin on his arms.

"Brock, so why did you need me in the first place?" James asked Brock who had just decided to roll out of bed.

"Oh yes, I went ridin' the other day, the Sheriff told me about the Whitmyre rustlers, and I took it upon myself, as always, and found out who they are."

"Who is it?"

"Ahem, Indians." He announced as he quickly but stealthily glanced over at Hiawatha.

"Indians?" James gasped.

"What tribe?" Hiawatha wondered leaning against the window staring out into the west.

"Shoshone!" Brock leaned back onto the two back legs of the dinner table chair.

"Why do they have to steal cattle?" James wondered, he thought that the Indians were given plenty of land to hunt. He pushed Brock's chair back onto four legs, that was his chair that Brock carelessly used.

"They're needy and badly need food. Ahem! I scooted my little self along to the camp of the biggest group of Shoshone Indians, without being seen mind you, and found that out. They starvin' James."

"James, what is the price for a head of cattle?" Hiawatha stood up, determination in his voice.

"I believe Mr. Whitmyre would sell one for eight dollars." James announced as he opened his closet door to grab a new black hat to replace the one he lost.

"I believe I will feed my people. Maybe with this I can win sonship back to my father."

"It will also stop the rustling." James said under his breath. "Hiawatha, we are brothers. And brothers stick together through the thick and thin, I'll buy them. You pay me back later. You worry about your father, and Hiawatha it might come to shooting to get out of the Indian camp alive, you know that; don't you?"

Hiawatha was just staring toward the west where he knew his tribe was.

"Agreed. Brother, I'm ready!"

Brock feeling left out again, pulled his hat over his eyes. He drew his piece of reed grass out of his hat band and began to chew on it. "And as for me I shall continue to sleep, for that seems to be all I know these last days with you gone." Brock jokingly started carefully putting his feet crossed on the table.

"Get up Brock. Come on!" James rolled his eyes and grabbed Brock by the arm.

"I'm coming, I'm coming!" Brock chuckled, as he was being dragged by James.

They mounted and headed straight for the ranch house. As they rode, James looked over at Hiawatha. He had a sense of happiness that James never knew the strong young Indian brave could possess. He watched him as he rode his white and tan pinto horse. On the rump of his horse, Hiawatha had put a blue hand print, which was the peace symbol of the Shoshone, and it was that that would get them safely through Shoshone Territory.

James signaled for the rest to stay behind as he rode up to the house. He bounded the steps, took off his hat, and knocked. Finally, after a while of waiting, Mr. Whitmyre came to the door.

"Hello James, sorry I was detained. Is something wrong?" He pulled out a chair for James to sit down but he remained standing.

"No, Nothing is wrong, I just need a favor."

"Anything James, I am always glad to help you with anything." He was stirring a cup of coffee.

"Well it's not me personally...you see we found out who was rustling." James fiddled with the brim of his black hat.

"You did? Who was it?" He was going for a sip of his coffee, but immediately put it down.

"Ahem, Indians."

"Indians? I haven't seen an Indian this side of the mountain in years." Mr. Whitmyre answered in disbelief.

"I know but it's true, what I want is to buy ten head of cattle. I want to bring the Indians some food. They're starvin' right now! Hiawatha is hoping he can be accepted back into the tribe if he saves his people from hunger. You see, it would do you good, it will stop the rustling." James tried to convince his boss.

"The cattle are yours, James; hands down. I just know I'm gonna kick myself in the seat, if the Indians get all the cattle, and then when winter comes along; they start rustling again."

"I will make the chief promise. From what Hiawatha says he is a good and upright leader."

"Alright. James you are a good young man. Five dollars a head."

"No, I'm gonna--"

"Five dollars a head and that's final."

"Thank you, Mr. Whitmyre." He fitted his hat back on and handed the money to his boss. After the transaction was completed, James and Hiawatha headed for the Sheriff's house; leaving Brock to choose the ten cattle and pick them out with the help of the other Whitmyre ranch hands.

"You know, James." Hiawatha yelled over the wind of them galloping along.

"Huh. A lot!"

"Hahaha! Noo, What I was going to say was that even though I'm a savage, I've learned one thing about you."

"Am I supposed to be terrified or is it okay to be relaxed?"

"A little of both is okay. Hahaha! No, I've just noticed that the Sheriffs house has been visited more frequently than usual lately."

"Is there a problem with that brother?"

"Oh No, No, No, No, nothing wrong with it at all. Just thought it was kind of interesting."

"I sure didn't know I was that obvious."

"Ha, my brother the mices and gophers of the wood couldn't help but know what was going on in your head." Hiawatha mocked James.

"Well I lived with them for ten years and got to know the Sheriff and Dorothy well." James tried to push it off with that excuse.

"Oh yeah, sure." Hiawatha didn't accept it at all.

They galloped until they reached the house. The Sheriff and his daughter were on the porch talking, when the two handsome riders rode up. They dismounted, Hiawatha looked over the back of his horse and whispered to James.

"Whatever you wanna do go ahead and do it." Hiawatha playfully winked over towards James.

"You know if I wasn't smart, I'd say you were getting a little in my business."

"Ain't that what brothers are for?" Hiawatha had a big smirk on his face.

"Yeah-, and about that, you been takin' that a little too far, now—"

"Hello, James." Dorothy called from the porch.

"Haha! The rocks they even cry out, how obvious you both are." Hiawatha rocked back laughing.

"Hello Sheriff." James threw his hand up and waved. Then he glared at Hiawatha, "Can you keep quiet for a change, savage!" The two laughed as they walked through the picket fence up to the Sheriff's house.

"How ya'll doin' this fine day?" The Sheriff asked as they walked up the steps.

"Doing well, Hiawatha here is gonna do a good deed for his tribe. We're gonna ride out and give his people some meat, they're starving. Brock found out that Hiawatha's people were rustling Whitmyre cattle. Hiawatha thinks maybe the cause of starvation is that there is no game in their lands anymore. They've been hunted very hard." James announced and said in quick beats.

"Really?" The Sheriff answered, "Wow I didn't think we'd ever hear of them Indians again, since they were put in their reservations. Good job, Hiawatha. Well come on inside, why do we stay out here in the broilin' heat?" The Sheriff opened the door to his house.

"Oh we just kinda, just dropped in to say hi that's all." James informed, as he started toward the steps.

"Nonsense," Dorothy squealed. "Come in, I just put coffee on the stove."

"I believe James would love to have warm fresh black coffee, wouldn't you?" Hiawatha with a smirk on his face, threw his big hand on James' shoulder.

"Coffee? Black. Oh yeah, coffee actually sounds good." James chuckled as he walked into the house behind the Sheriff, and Hiawatha followed.

They entered the house and Dorothy had already set the cups out and set next to it homemade donuts; James' favorite. James looked over at Hiawatha, Hiawatha was looking around at the very elaborate and decorative dwelling of the Sheriff. He walked over to the fireplace, where two seats sat opposite each other, a board sat in the middle, painted on the board were red and black squares, with round objects on the board. Hiawatha played as though he could not figure out what it was. Dorothy noticed the perplexed Indian and walked up to him.

"You know what that is?" She asked as she dried off her hands on a towel.

"Ha no actually I don't know, looks weird...I take it that its some game."

"Yeah it's a game; here I'll show you." She chuckled as she sat on the opposite chair and motioned for him to take the other.

"Now these are my pieces and those are yours." She gathered the black and pushed the reds to him.

"What is this game called?" Hiawatha asked ignorantly.

"Checkers."

"Oh-okay."

"Now what you're supposed to do is...." She kept on explaining to Hiawatha the rules of the game of checkers. Hiawatha glanced over his shoulder to James and grinned. Hiawatha knew checkers, he had learned the game in the white man's school. "That poor old meddlesome Injun can't keep his mind off me or my business." James thought to himself. But he did take this opportunity to find the Sheriff.

The Sheriff had gone into his home office and had been looking at some papers when James walked in.

"Oh hey James, just thought I'd come back here and get some business done. You need anything?"

"No, well actually yes, Ahem, a little of both, but definitely more of the yes." James stammered and stuttered like a train rolling off the tracks and grinding rails trying to get back on.

"James, are you okay? Is something wrong?"

"Nothing's wrong, Sheriff. I just wanted to come and, you know, thank you for raising me since my family died. Someday I hope to repay you for all that you did for me."

"Nonsense! You are like a son to me, you owe me nothing."

"Thank you!" James replied not sure how to ask the next question on his mind.

"Somethin' else is running through your mind, isn't it?"

"Kinda sorta!" He stopped staring at the pile of papers on the Sheriff's desk, then what he wanted to say just came out. "Sheriff, I love Dorothy, and I would like if it I could have your permission to marry her soon."

"James, my son! I knew this was coming a long way off, and I have prayed that it would be reality, you have my blessing."

The Sheriff stood, and they embraced; after, James asked if it could be kept a secret until the right day, the Sheriff agreed and they both walked into the room where Hiawatha and Dorothy were still playing checkers. Dorothy was having fun teaching a game to an Indian, but Hiawatha was tired of playing the game already. They spent a couple of hours there, and then they headed for Brock.

A little later after their visit, James again met Brock and had him hire ten men to start to drive the herd over the mountain to the Indian tribe. James and Hiawatha helped herd the cattle into the corrals, so they could be ready to go when it was time.

After their business was settled, James and Hiawatha started making their way to the Indian tribe, first, before the herd of cattle.

It was about a two-hour ride to the tribe's encampment, and with night quickly approaching, they stopped in the forest right outside a town called Cody. Before the sun set, they built a decent size campfire and had supper. They sat around the campfire and talked a little while about their lives. James made his mat with his bedroll and put his saddle for a pillow.

As he lay there, James pulled out his bible from his jacket and began to read. He opened to Psalms 24; and he read his favorite psalm. A passage of power and the majesty of God. After Hiawatha had come back from washing the dishes in the river, he saw James reading his bible.

"You carry a bible with you?" Hiawatha asked as he threw the dishes onto a small deerskin that they used to wrap them.

"Everywhere I go!" James said matter-of-factly.

"I was taught some things about the bible when I was in school. I don't know...I've thought long about the possibility of a great deity." Hiawatha pulled on the fringe of his buckskin as he talked.

"Hiawatha. I understand and know that where you came from; your background, your peoples' religion is different. But there is a great God in heaven; the one who created all things. There are many things we as human beings don't and can't understand. But God has given each and every human being a way to know about this great being that could and should be our Lord......I was just reading in Psalms. Listen." And James read his cherished psalm.

The earth is the LORD'S, and the fulness thereof; the world, and they that dwell therein. For he hath founded it upon the seas, and established it upon the floods. Who shall ascend into the hill of the LORD? or who shall stand in his holy place? He that hath clean hands, and a pure heart; who hath not lifted up his soul unto vanity, nor sworn deceitfully. He shall receive the blessing from the LORD, and righteousness from the God of his salvation. This is the generation of them that seek him, that seek thy face, O Jacob. Selah. Lift up your heads, O ye gates; and be ye lift up, ye everlasting doors; and the King of glory shall come in. Who is this King of glory? The LORD strong and mighty, the LORD mighty in battle. Lift up your heads, O ye gates; even lift them up, ye everlasting doors; and the King of glory shall come in. Who is this King of glory? The LORD of hosts, he is the King of glory. Selah.

"Powerful." Hiawatha muttered under his breath, but so that James could hear him.

"I know, and it's the truth. Hiawatha, he will receive every human being that comes to him. Goodnight, Bro." James knowing that he had stirred something in his red brother's heart, decided to leave it there for the night. He stuffed his bible in his jacket, then pulled his covers over him, and soon was asleep.

8

The next morning, Hiawatha woke up to a soft noise and a little chirp. He quietly lifted his head and looked and there was a small and frail, quail pecking at the ground. Hiawatha pulled out his knife slowly and quietly; the little quail jumped and pecked at the ground unaware of its predator. Hiawatha slowly and carefully took aim, and then quickly threw his knife. His aim was true, he jumped up and grabbed the flapping bird.

"Ha-ha." He chuckled to himself then turned to the sleeping James. "James, look what wandered into our camp this morning? A breakfast fit for a king!"

"Nice job." He said yawning, he turned over and then he saw the tiny dead bird. It looked so tiny and frail, hanging from Hiawatha's hand, he could not believe Hiawatha expected them both to eat that little bird. "QUAIL?" He screeched. "What's that supposed to feed? You possibly expect that thing to fill me up?" He sat up a little perturbed at the breakfast he was about to have.

"Fear not, friend James. There's plenty for everyone." Hiawatha said laughing, as he started to skin the unlucky bird.

"Yeah, maybe to feed every ant in the county; but not to feed us grown up men! I'm going to the river to see if there is anything there; maybe a couple minnows!" James rolled his eyes and marched off; Hiawatha laughing heartily.

Moments later, James came walking back to the campsite, empty handed; Hiawatha was laid back next to the fallen log he had slept against. James saw him, then looked over and saw the half-eaten quail still on the spigot over the small fire. He walked up to the fire and noticed that Hiawatha had graciously left the two legs of the tiny bird. He pulled them off and walked to his mat and plopped down. Ravenously, pulling apart the legs with his teeth, he glanced over at Hiawatha in the corner of his eye, and Hiawatha was staring at him. Hiawatha saw him glance and laughed a hearty laugh.

"Would you quit laughing at me?" James threw the already eaten legs behind him. "Boy, I'm still hungry." He muttered under his breath.

Hiawatha chuckled. "Well, we must be off." He stood to his feet, rubbing his hands on his arms.

"Yeaah! Well first after that unique and elaborate meal fit for a termite, I gotta wash my hands in the river." James started off.

"What a waste! You should just rub your hands onto your arms to let all the oils of your meal get into your skin. It's good for your skin!"

"Ahem, Well, like I was saying, I gotta wash my hands in the river." James went to turn and tripped on a root sticking up out of the ground and fell. He got up and walked to the river not far off.

"Haahaha!" Boomed the Indian, he loved mocking and joking around with his white brother.

After they had finished picking up camp, they headed up the mountain. Soon they topped the mountain and there it was in the valley, the camp of the once proud Shoshone, a green forest with smoke rising from it. Just over the mountain was a great wilderness, known as the Yellowstone, with geysers and hot springs. The Indian dwellers stayed away from the geysers and hot springs, believing that to be the lands where the great spirit expresses his wrath to the world. As they approached closer, Hiawatha instructed, and they put blue hand prints on their horses' rumps, indicating that they came in peace. In the mountains around them, they looked and saw smoke signals.

"James, look." He pointed to the signals. "They knew we were coming from miles away."

"Wow." James tried to sound impressed.

"Indians have the senses of an animal." Hiawatha nudged his horse forward, James just shrugged his shoulders and followed.

After a few miles, they came to a wood clearing, which lined the Indian camp; down deeper in the valley was the main camp of the Shoshone.

"James, this is where we must part." Hiawatha announced as he pulled the reigns of his horse to a complete stop.

"Part? What, you're not coming?" James turned around in his saddle, looking at Hiawatha.

"I have to know if I can be forgiven before I can walk in there. Its death if I ride in there otherwise...."

"Death? What about me?" James screeched pointing to his chest.

"They won't kill you immediately, because you have the symbol. They respect it too much, but I must tell you some things first...for starter, my father is the chief."

"Chief?" James dropped his mouth open in amazement, but Hiawatha continued on. "His name is Chief Washakie.

"Oh Was-ake. I heard of him some place!" James failed to pronounce the chiefs' name right.

Hiawatha threw his head back, holding the reins of his horse. "James, to speak to an Indian especially an Indian chief, you must speak with respect especially if you wanna keep your hide."

"My hide! Oh yes, that's something that I've had for a long time, I wouldn't wanna lose it now!" James chuckled, totally not joking.

"And the first thing is to pronounce the chief's name correctly, it is Wa-sha-kie!" Hiawatha took the name apart for James to remember.

"Wasss. Ahem, Washakie. Washakie." James repeated the name over and over again hoping not to forget it.

"Ask Chief Washakie concerning me; if negative run for your life, if positive fire three shots in the air, and I'll come."

"Run for my life...I like the sound of that!" James nodded and shook hands with his red brother;

Hiawatha gave him some other rules and steps to go by, and then he rode on down the mountain. James passed one scout, then another, then another, each just staring at him not knowing what to do; he slowly cantered until he was inside the camp. The Indians stared in surprise at this unannounced visitor, first because he showed no fear, but second because he had the Shoshone symbol of peace on his horse's hindquarters. As he rode, James looked at the children who were starving, he could tell that they hadn't eaten in a long time. He kept riding till he got to the place Hiawatha had told him to stop, James dismounted and stood in front of an old Indian, it was the chief and his name was, Chief Washakie.

With his heart beating rapidly, he approached the chief. "Chief Wa-Washakie?" James asked not sure if the old man understood him, tipping his hat.

"I am he...speak!" The Indian with arms folded had on a gloomy face, one that looked like it had a dark cloud over it.

"Ahem, I am James Cassidy. I come to the chief's tepee in peace, as a friend of the Shoshone."

"You, James Cassidy is welcome, you bear the peace symbol of the Shoshone, Welcome."

"Thank you. Chief Wa – um, Chief. I come first with a petition, then a gift to your tribe."

"Speak on."

James standing in front of his horse still holding the reins, glanced around uneasy at the crowd that gathered, then began to speak. "I have travelled long and far, I live in Burlington; some town a couple hours from here. And, umm, one day miraculously, I met a man, he was a good man; he and I, through these last few weeks have become close friends, we've actually become brothers. This man offended your tribe and was sent away. He wants and desires forgiveness and readmittance back into his people, for he loves them. That man is Hiawatha, your son."

"Hiawatha? My son?" The chief stared at James, joy filling his old face, he lifted his hands to grab James but stayed.

"It is, and this is the token he sent along with me to show you." He pulled out of his shirt pocket a necklace, it had the claw of a Grizzly bear and engraved on the claw was two hands holding each other's.

"It is my son!" He showed a face of happiness and joy, but as quick as it had appeared it disappeared, and the great chief had a face that shook James to his toes. Suddenly, the chief slapped James and he fell to the ground. And before James could get up, twelve spears leveled down toward him. He went onto his elbows, the chief motioned for them to lift their spears away.

"Up, get on your horse, and go." He motioned for them to bring him his horse.

"And why all of a sudden this change of heart?" He asked as he slowly stood to his feet, brushing himself off.

"You try to mock me, to bring my son's memory back to me. Leave!"

"Now chief you listen here..." James pointed his finger at the man, to try to convince him.

"I've had enough!" He walked into the tepee behind him. James started to go in there, but two warriors dropped their spears in front of the door. "OH, so this is how ya'll play this game? Alright." With that, James grabbed both spears and pulled them apart. The two braves fought to try to stop him, but after James punched the first one and kicked the other one in the stomach, he turned to the crowd; his hands spread apart ready for anything, but in that last show of power he had managed to gain the respect of his audience. He quickly turned and grabbed the tepee flaps and walked in. The old chief Washakie was facing the opposite wall, smoking on his peace pipe.

"Now you listen here, chief Wes...wash...wa, whatever; I didn't just come down here to get slapped by an old chief or-or come to start a fight. But I am most certainly and most definitely going to finish what I came to do. Chief, your son is innocent!"

"Talk, I'll listen. Just once!" The chief turned and faced James and set his pipe down.

"Well, Hiawatha as an innocent child, was sleeping in his father's tent. He woke from the hoot of an owl, or the howl of a timber wolf, something in the deep woods of night woke him up. So, he then walked out of his tepee, to get a bit of fresh air and to look at the stars. When two men snuck in and kidnapped him, and took him deep into the woods, they tied him to a tree. And told him that if he did not show them where the yellow iron flows through the land of the Indian they would kill him. They held a knife to his throat; and even then, your son didn't say anything. They started to beat him, still he said nothing. It wasn't until they pulled out a gun and said they would shoot him and kill others of the tribe, that he broke and told. The white men are the guilty ones. Would you forgive your son, Wasakie? He is a true Shoshone brave!"

The old man now had tears in his eyes; he glared down at the ground as he spoke.

"You are a great chief, known throughout the whole country. Among red and white alike, will the chief make a wise decision, regarding his own son?"

"Hiawatha. Where is he?" He looked up from his deep meditation.

"He waits my signal. Is he welcome back with his people?" James asked a little bit of desperation in his tone.

"Yes. I have grieved ever since I sent him away. My heart now is thrilled, though some in my tribe would not. Yes, bring my son back to me."

James jumped up and walked outside, he fired three shots in the air. The crowd of Shoshone Indians jumped at the sudden gun bursts. The chief walked out of his tepee, holding his coup staff, to see his long-lost son. In a matter of minutes, miraculously and out of nowhere, Hiawatha appeared on the wood line. A glorious picture to every eye that gazed on him. His white pinto reared back on his hind hoofs and whinnied. The horse was an icon of beauty with his tail waving in the breeze that went through the valley. Hiawatha had gone down to the creek and painted his face. With blue stripes running down the sides of his face into his neck, symbolizing Family and Unity, to the Shoshones. Also, white dots scattered his cheeks and forehead, representing Love and Compassion. His stallion was almost as charming as its rider, Hiawatha had painted a black ring around his right eye, symbolizing Victory and Luck. He painted long red zig-zags down the length of his horses' front legs, as a call to the great spirit to give him Speed and Endurance.

His appearance mesmerized the whole camp as he sat on his horse and gazed on his people for a few seconds. He sat taking in all his surroundings, he knew some would be glad to see him, and some would not. The sight brought the chief to an abundance of tears; and then the mighty young brave kicked his horse in the flanks and started moving into the camp. His father watched as his son came riding in; not only handsome and strong, but in every way, it was the very image of *his* son. Hiawatha rode at a brisk trot, he looked at his people, long missed but not forgotten. He rode past many tepees, and many tribesmen, but as he passed one of the dwellings a young Indian girl stood at the open flap of her teepee, gazing at him. Hiawatha slowed his horse down, the two locked eyes with each

other; and within a matter of seconds he heeled his horse and trotted off. He rode up to his father, threw his leg over the horse's back, and stood in front of his father. Chief Washakie looked into his son's eyes, they joined hands, and for a long time they held onto each other's arms; and then they embraced.

The Indian audience that had been watching; shouted and started to chant. For they knew that this great chief, both to the white man and Indian, had missed his son ever since his departure. The crowd was happy for the chief and his son, save for one who was standing in the front, the chiefs nephew, Hiawatha's cousin, Etu.

"My son, My son." The chief repeated as he held Hiawatha close. The world knows no joy that that Indian chief displayed in front of his tepee that cloudy afternoon.

"Prepare a feast, for we will feast tonight. Hiawatha and his friend will celebrate this night with us."

They feasted with all the food they had; for it was a worthy cause of celebration, the old chief joined in the dancing and the pleasures of the night. James and Hiawatha sat and watched the excitement of the evening; then after a signal, all stopped. Chief Washakie walked towards Hiawatha, followed by two squaws carrying a warbonnet. Hiawatha stood and the warbonnet was placed on his head. The medicine man then came and danced around and around Hiawatha muttering and chanting. Hiawatha stood like a statute, arms folded against his chest and staring into unknown. Just then the old medicine man spoke, "May the gods that chose to bring you back among us, keep you safe in the land where you now dwell." After the medicine man had walked off Hiawatha began to speak.

"My people, I am happy to be a part of my people again; my heart is glad. I have good news for you. I have heard of the hunger that you face; I also know that young Indian brave go and steal white man's cattle. The white man not happy, they say, Indian must stop stealing white man's cattle. Chief Washakie, I have ten cattle that will feed this camp for a while, they will be here at dawn. It will provide food for your children and yourselves, until the woods replenish, and we can hunt for our own."

And then it was when the Shoshone brave, Etu stood up and began to curse Hiawatha. "Cattle? Since when has our blood, that flows through our veins, changed to that of the white man's? We are not farmers, we are hunters. We will take no gifts from this dog, the traitor of our people." Etu had a face of rage as he spoke.

Hiawatha stood up fast, anger in his eyes, he ran up to Etu and punched him in the face. Etu went flying back, he stood up, his lip bleeding. He drew his knife and lunged for Hiawatha. Hiawatha ducked and tripped Etu. Etu went sprawling onto the ground. Hiawatha jumped on Etu's back and pulled the offending arm behind him and held him in a lock position. Etu groaned from the pain that Hiawatha inflicted to his arm. Hiawatha took Etus' knife and held it at Etu's throat.

"Listen, Etu. I am not nor ever was a traitor. I spare your life this time, but not ever again will you try to stir up trouble like that. And don't you ever, ever call me a traitor." Etu wriggled to get free.

"As I was saying before I was so rudely interrupted," He resumed his conversation with the crowd as he got off Etu and returned his knife. Etu stomped off, away from the crowd, followed by two other braves. "The cattle will be herded down the valley tomorrow and left where the river turns toward the east. We'll need some men to help us."

Some of the people didn't like the thought of taking gifts, but Hiawatha put it to them as rustling, they will just happen to find the cattle grazing by the river. When the crowd heard it put like that they were eager to help and help they did.

After the feast was over, Chief Washakie showed Hiawatha and James an unoccupied tepee that they could spend the night. They accepted, and soon was all rolled out and laid down.

"How do you feel, Hiawatha?" James asked as he stared out the hole in the top of their tepee, watching the stars.

"I feel great, I thought this day would never come." He sighed as he spoke.

"I know what you mean. What's up with that Etu guy?"

"He would have become chief after my father, he is my father's closest nephew. But since I am returned and accepted, he has lost it."

"Oh, so that is why he attacked you."

"Yes. Greed, greed."

"Huh. Well goodnight. Tomorrow is a big day already."

"Indeed, goodnight."

The two slept soundly. A few hours later, James woke up to a noise. He lay staring through the black, he knew the noise was too weird to be just 'anything', so he laid there not moving. He strained his ears to try to hear. Ghostly, the tepee flap began to open, and then the face of an Indian appeared. James kicked Hiawatha's feet to wake him up. Hiawatha woke and saw the intruder, "Etu." He muttered. Suddenly the silhouette sprang onto Hiawatha, as the dark figure sprang through the air, James caught glimpse of a knife. "Hiawatha!" Hiawatha avoided the knife, he grabbed the intruder by the arm and kicked him in the face. Etu went flying backwards right onto James,

"Hey!!" James voice was drowned out by Etus' body being slammed against him. "Thanks Bro." James pushed the Indian off and pinned him to the ground.

"Etu?" James squealed, looking up at Hiawatha. "Boy, he wasn't born to fight. That was to easy!"

"Etu!" Hiawatha confirmed. James grabbed Etu by his leather tan-hide jacket and pulled him up.

"You have tried to come and kill me while I slept, Etu? That is the way of a squaw. Now listen to me, tomorrow at dawn we will climb Cody Peak, and there we will fight. We will see who the great spirit allows to live; if you are man enough, Etu." Hiawatha challenged Etu.

"Tomorrow dawn!" Etu stormed out of the tepee.

James watched as Etu walked out; he looked back at Hiawatha. Hiawatha wore a queer and sullen face.

"I haven't even been here a full day and I already have an appointment to kill one of my own people." Hiawatha turned away and clenched his right fist.

"Man!" James scratched his head, combing his hair back with his fingers as he spoke. "I sure don't take to killin', but for someone to come and try to kill you while you slept...I don't know, but that would be a pretty big indicator to me that he's gotta go."

They laid there not going back to sleep. A couple hours later, as the sun began to rise in the east, Hiawatha got up and prepared for his appointment.

"I think I should be there just in case something goes wrong." James said, rubbing his eyes.

"No by the custom of my people, two go into the mountain alone...only one returns." Hiawatha said, as he knelt to crawl out of the tepee.

"Gnaa!" James noised, he was buckling his gun-belt, as he heard what Hiawatha said, 'only one returns.'

James and Hiawatha walked together to where a group of men were standing. The chief had been summoned to appear before the fight. The chief, the medicine man, Etu's Father, and a few other men, sat on their horses in the middle of the road which led to Cody's Peak. Hiawatha and Etu stood in front of their elders. The medicine man slid off his horse and walked to the two young men.

"Hum, hum, hum, eta, eta, bum, bum." The man chanted as he approached shaking a rattling gourd. He tied a leather strap that was about ten feet long tightly to Hiawatha's wrist, he took the other end and secured it to Etu's wrist also.

"You will walk far where the cry of battle cannot be heard by others. You will climb where only the eyes

93

of the great spirit can see. You will remain until one of you returns to earth. Go!" he commanded. They were given two knives, then they took off. The two raced up the mountain, side by side. James sent a prayer to heaven and asked for God's mercy in that hour.

Hiawatha and Etu ran about half a mile and reached the top of Cody's Peak. When they made it to the top, they stood and stared at each other. Nose to nose they defiantly stared at each other. Hiawatha spoke.

"I've learned one thing in the years that I have lived on this earth; greed, jealousy, and pride get people into more trouble than anything else. We stand here now to fight each other, because someone was jealous and greedy. And had come to the point where he would kill his own cousin."

With that Etu angrily using his first burst of power and strength, jerked on the leather strap, sending Hiawatha flying towards him, Etu raised his knife and hit him in the forehead with the butt of his knife. Hiawatha fell back and spun away, landing on his stomach. He held his head, the first blow and he was bleeding, blood flowed down his hand and down his arm. He slowly got up, and Etu went to pull it again. But this time Hiawatha ran for him, which made Etu go off balance. Hiawatha then seizing his opportunity, put all his might into throwing Etu. Etu went spinning, out of control, as Hiawatha pulled and threw all his weight on the strap. Uncontrolled, Etu went slamming against the rock wall. With a cry of pain, he bent backwards, holding his back that was in excruciating pain, he dropped, Hiawatha waited for him to get his head clear again,

while he held his own bleeding head. Etu stood and stumbled to Hiawatha, and then with a frantic thrust he went to stab him; but Hiawatha dodged and kicked him in the backend, sending him straight to the ground. Hiawatha then went to jump on top of him; but before he reached him, Etu spun and kicked Hiawatha in the stomach as he was coming down. Hiawatha flew backwards and did a flip and fell next to him: dizzy and disoriented. Etu then pounced onto the weakening Hiawatha; and held his knife close to his chest, Hiawatha held the knife away pushing with all his might. Having Etu's wrist with both of his hands, he used every last ounce of strength he had, and flipped Etu off of him. Enraged, Etu jumped up and jerked Hiawatha to him.

In the sudden jolt, Hiawatha's knife fell out of his hand and dropped to the ground. Before Hiawatha could do anything, Etu rapped the strap around Hiawatha's neck. Now in this moment Hiawatha was in desperate trouble; he was being choked to death. He pulled at Etu's arms to get free, he pinched and clawed at the arms of his conquering opponent, but he was locked and was going to die. His mind went nowhere and thought of nothing save his last conversation with his white brother; the talk they had of that Great Spirit. He had never accepted the fact of the Son of God that came and shed his own blood for his soul. But in that moment as he faced death, he saw it plain and clear. He prayed the only way he knew, praying and pleading to the God of his white brother that he would save his soul.

In that moment he had an inspiration; he went limp acting as though he were dead, Etu let him loose thinking he had won and was going to sink his knife into Hiawatha to finish his work. In an instant, Hiawatha grabbed his knife that had fallen on the ground and spun, stood, and struck Etu in the heart. Etu grabbed his chest, blood flowing from his deep, fatal wound, he looked at Hiawatha, then squeezing his eyes tight. He dropped to his knees and fell on his back. Faintly losing consciousness and full of pain, he tried to get up. Sympathy and regret swept over Hiawatha as he ran over and knelt beside the dying Etu; putting his arm around his head, he gathered every scrap of material on Etu and tried to stop the bleeding.

"Kill me, Hiawatha, finish it!" Etu laid in shock, swinging between life and death in Hiawatha's arms,

"No, Etu. I had no desire to kill my own flesh and blood. I regret your greedy thoughts and desires. But I will not end your life any more than I already did. The great God in heaven will decide whether you live or die." Hiawatha kneeling there did all he could do for his dying cousin. Etu grabbed Hiawatha's arm and tried to pull himself up.

"I saw you with the chiefs own warbonnet. And worse yet, I saw you, the future chief sitting in the seat of the young chiefs, a place I dreamed of taking the day you left the tribe. And when you came back I was filled with hatred and greed. I thought I could kill you Hiawatha, your knife was true, mine was evil." Etu grabbed Hiawatha's arm. "Forgive me, Hiawatha, my chief." Etu then went limp in Hiawatha's arms, Etu laid there motionless. Hiawatha wept deeply, great sobs bubbled from his heart. His sorrow for Etu rushed out in a river of tears. He held his hands over his face, as his whole body shook with deep heavy sobs.

"For dust thou art, and unto dust shalt thou return." Hiawatha muttered as he wept; blood and tears streamed down his face.

Hiawatha picked up Etu and brought him away to a private place and buried him along with his war knife, using a pile of rocks. Hiawatha grabbed his own knife used in the combat and with a bit of rage threw it over the mountain side with all his might. He stood over the grave of Etu and sang the funeral song of the Shoshone.

"Woa-ooo-ahhh. _Yooae-ahhhh! Wy-oottaa!"

After he respectfully gave the dead its due, he descended the mountain, and was met by James and the anxious spectators.

"Hiawatha. Praise God. You've been spared." James went to join hands with his brother, but Hiawatha didn't notice.

"Good men sell their lives to greed, jealousy, and pride...and end up dying like Etu."

"Hiawatha, I believe God has spared your life for a particular purpose." James put his hand on his red brother's shoulder.

"Brother, I don't know what you happen to be talking about right now, but I do know of some cattle that need to be rustled." A squaw ran up and gave Hiawatha a bowl of water to wash his face.

9

It was now August of 1884, two months after his visit to the camp of the now happy Shoshone. When he arrived back in Burlington he started building his new house, he desired to make it like the dreamhouse his father always wanted. He centered the foundation right where his childhood house had stood; the grim black pile now forever gone.

Two weeks went by, and by this time, he had the whole frame up, and was starting the roof. One day as he was alone on the roof, a group of ten Indians came riding over the hill. Hiawatha led the Indians to James house.

"Brother James!" Hiawatha yelled to James up on the roof.

"Hiawatha, what brings ya way out here?" James asked as he tossed his hammer to the ground.

"Well, Indians don't know a thing about putting a house together, but we thought you would need help putting the roof on, and in a hurry." Hiawatha motioned for the other braves to dismount.

"Thanks for the help, but why the hurry?"

"Rain! Much rain! Indian scouts that live in the mountain tops, gave signals that rain is coming and coming quickly."

"Oh... well then, thank you brother."

Before two hours had passed, the sky became dark and the sun disappeared behind the clouds. The roof was quickly put on before the big storm, and James was the last one on the roof, he stood there and gazed at the sky. "This one is gonna be a big'un!" he thought to himself.

"James, the sky will start lighting up in a minute. You better start considering the option of coming down." Hiawatha yelled his horse prancing back and forth under him.

As if in answer to Hiawatha, the sky let out a giant thunderbolt which shook all the bystanders. A little startled, James just jumped off the roof and fell to the ground, he got up and walked over to Hiawatha.

"As I was saying..." Hiawatha laughed as he spoke to James.

"Yeah, I just might oughta start listening to you more of'en!" James mockingly winked at Hiawatha.

By the next week, James had finished his house. A simple log cabin, with a porch that covered the full front length of the house, borne up by six cedar posts. A lonely rocking chair and a porch swing rocked back and forth with the mild western breeze. A stone chimney stood on both ends of the house, with no smoke coming from their flues. The roof was covered in shingle slates, tightly fitted together, and in a unified pattern. The porch, only one step off the ground was solid and spacious. The front door stood wide open as if to welcome anyone who entered.

Inside the humble dwelling, a woodstove sat to the left, a dishtowel hanging from its handle. A fireplace stood in the living room, on the wall above the fireplace hung a set of deer antlers, on the floor next to fireplace a mountain lion head and skin; the same taxidermy that decorated his first home. As he stood inside his house that evening he breathed a sigh of satisfaction and relief. He anticipated showing his new home to his first visitors, special visitors.

Evening was dwindling as James rode up to the Sheriff's house, he hadn't seen any of them since the day before Hiawatha's fight with Etu; for he was busy on his surprise. He quietly dismounted and tiptoed his way to the gate. He went to open the little gate; it squeaked as it had always done.

"Confounded gate!" he muttered to himself, he didn't remember it being that loud.

"James! I thought you'd never come back, I haven't seen you in weeks where you been?" Dorothy came out the door and stared anxiously at James. They stopped before they entered.

"That sis', is a long story!" He exclaimed as he opened the door and motioned for her to enter.

"James how...where you been son?" The Sheriff stood up with a little concern in his voice.

"A lot has happened since I saw you last," James sat down and told them everything. He told them about Hiawatha's acceptance back into his tribe, he told them about the fight and how Hiawatha had won, he told them everything. As his story came to an end, he exclaimed.

"Oh, by the way, I have a surprise for the both of you..." He stood up. "Feel like riding out to my farm?"

"Sure...sure." They nodded in agreement. They rose up, the Sheriff buckled on his gun-belt, as Dorothy went for her tan shawl. Soon they boarded the Sheriffs' buckboard and James rode his black quarter horse and were soon heading out to James' farm.

As they reached the farm night had just fallen; and it wasn't until James had lit his bonfire pile, were they able to see Jame's surprise.

"You built your house, so that's what you been doing all this time?" Dorothy exclaimed, the wind blowing strands of hair that escaped from under her bonnet

"James, this is just like what your father wanted. He detailed it to me many years ago, did he ever tell you?" The Sheriff stated, also remembering that it was his last conversation with James father.

"Never details. But he always told me the kind of house he liked." James answered both hands on his hips, resting on his belt.

"It is so nice. Can we go in?" Dorothy anxiously asked.

"Oh-yeah sure, I guess, we can go in." James stuttered, he gave a look to the Sheriff, and the Sheriff knew exactly what he meant.

"I'll be right in after I, umm-ahem, tie the horses." The Sheriff said with a little more than a gleam in his eye.

"'Kay, pa." Dorothy responded as she walked toward the house, followed by James, hands in his back pockets.

As they entered, James walked to the other side of the room and lit the fireplace. And a few candles to light up the room, he hung his hat on his hook by the door and stood at the table. Dorothy walked around the room and examined the place.

"It's lovely, James, very nice!" Dorothy announced, with her back to James. She stood toying with one of James' window curtains.

"I know...wo-wel, - I mean thank you! Thank you!" James stammered his mind was in a different place. He was tongue-tied and didn't know how to start the conversation he was wanting to begin.

"Is this house nice enough for you to want to live in it?" James asked, a few moments later, as he went to sit on the table top.

"What do you mean?" She asked, as she spun around and faced James.

"Dorothy, we've known each other for years; like brother and sister. But now I'd like to ask you something special......Will you marry me?"

Dorothy was more or less shocked, for that had been her heart for a long time. But now that the time had come she found herself speechless. She gazed into James eyes, and quietly answered James.

"Yes, I will, James!" James with a sigh of relief and thankfulness, turned to the door to tell the Sheriff he could come in, but strangely enough he was coming in the door.

"Pa, me and James are getting married." Dorothy announced in a content voice.

"You are?" The Sheriff ignorantly asked.

"Yes..." Dorothy had just supposed her father had already known.

"I know, I'm playin' with ya. He asked me awhile back. That was one reason I knew he was a' comin' back!" The Sheriff, James, and Dorothy now laughed a pure heartfelt laughter.

Dorothy and James, side by side started walking towards the buggy; the Sheriff mounted James horse.

"Uhh wha-what?" James hesitatingly asked.

"Well seeins' that I ain't the one getting married to Dorothy, I think you should be the one ridin' with her...might have some things to talk about." The Sheriff winked at Dorothy and rode off, not too fast though. James and Dorothy rode behind in the buckboard following the Sheriff's dust, and soon were home.

10

A couple days later, James awoke to the noise of someone knocking at the door. He buttoned up his shirt and walked to the door.

"Brock! Hey where you been?" James held his hand over his still sleepy eyes from the bright morning sun.

"I think the question should be, where have you been, nit-wit?"

"Wait...That's the same question. Hahaha! Without the nit-wit. Its real good to see you again."

"As it is you, my friend. So, which brings me back to my first question, where have you been?" Brock asked again.

So, James got two cups of coffee and gave one to Brock and sat down and told him everything that happened, that is, everything except his recent proposal.

"Wow sounds like you had a very interesting few months. But I'm afraid that your adventure has only begun. You see, I've been doing my own hunting these last couple months." Brock announced as he drummed his fingers on the table.

"What do you mean?" James asked, for Brock spoke as if he had a burden.

Just as Brock began to speak, a rider came riding towards his house.

"Tarnation!" Brock slapped the table with an open hand. "I can never sit down and tell you anything we always get interrupted. We always get interrupted by senseless Yahoos!" Brock rubbed his palm, the slap from the table stung his hand.

James laughed and opened the door. It was the Sheriff's youngest deputy.

"Hello Jack. What brings ya way out here?" James pulled the brim of his hat to shadow his eyes, shielding them from the morning sun.

"James. The bank was robbed last night, everything is gone. Money, banknotes, gold, everything. The Sheriff told me to ride out and get you to ride posse with him. He needs everyman he can get."

"How many thieves you figure?" James asked, he was not expecting his day to start out like this.

"Well that's the complicated part, we counted four riders. But the strangest thing, from some evidence we found, is it seems to be the work of a gang." The deputy answered.

"Alright I'm coming. I'll meet him in the meadow at Snake River." James stated as he had already turned back to his house to get some last-minute items.

"Yep!" The deputy turned as he sped off in a hurry.

"Well Brock, your town gossip will have to wait."

"Oh, no it don't, I'm going along too." Brock said straightforward.

"Alright. I'm sure we'll find the time!" chuckled James as he tightened the saddle on his quarter horse. Brock rode off to beat James to Snake River Meadow.

Just then the sound of a galloping rider came riding over the hill. James turned squinting in the sunlight, he focused on the rider, and his heart gave a leap for joy; Hiawatha was riding in.

"Hiawatha. It's good to see ya friend. Why ya way out here?" James jumped onto his horse and rode up to Hiawatha.

"Is there a law, that says Indians can't see their friends. Ha! No, first of all, I came to make sure you are still in one piece. Which is always first and foremost! Second, to invite you to an Indian wedding."

"Indian wedding. Well dog-on-it! That sounds interesting. Who you marrying?"

"Who said it had to be me?"

"Me!" James announced not giving Hiawatha a time to reply.

"Oh well you're right for once. It will take place on the second full moon. You'll come!"

"Why would I miss it? Funny cause I proposed last night to Dorothy too."

"Proposed?"

"Uhm yeah, I asked if she would marry me. So, we'll be getting married soon too. If everything goes right! Right now, I gotta go ride posse with the Sheriff. Why don't you come along? That is, unless you got weddin' bells to hang in some trees."

"What are you waitin' for?" Hiawatha slapped his horse and sped away, James before long taking the lead.

They rode away and after some time finally met the Sheriff at Snake River meadow and started tracking the bank robbers. There was a group of about four horse track pairs. They followed them till they came through a wide and spacious canyon where they could tell the pursued outlaws had camped. At a small campfire, Brock knelt down and felt the ash.

"Not more than four hours old." He declared and then remounted his horse.

They continued following the tracks eight miles south of town, which led into a small desert, there they could tell the robbers had stopped again. But this time, eighteen other tracks were joined to the four from the east; and they left together. They headed straight north in the direction of Burlington.

The Sheriff and James sat staring at the tracks, then in unison looked up at Brock and Hiawatha, who were both staring towards Burlington.

"Now what do you make of that?" James asked looking back down at the many hoof prints going every which way.

"Boy, now they're a giant force, our group of fifteen men might not be a match for them." The Sheriff said also examining the tracks, hands on his hips.

"Why did they cut straight for town? It's just about ten miles in that direction." James pointed to the north.

"My friend, they're wanting more than what they took from the bank; they're wanting Burlington." Brock kneeled on the ground.

"What do you mean?" James walked towards Brock.

"I mean that when you make it back to Burlington. You are going to find it guarded by twenty-two outlaws." Brock announced, kneeling on one knee, bracing himself with his elbow on the other.

"How do you come to this conclusion?" The Sheriff asked, for Brock had answered the question in his own mind.

Brock jumped and stood on his horse's back, so he could have a better advantage of viewing farther and looked with his hands over his eyes. "I see a great cloud of dust way off in the distance about six miles away, heading towards Burlington...Ah-oh," Brock remarked as he realized another small cloud of dust. "They have three scouts lagging behind about four miles away." Brock jumped off his horse and patted his mare's neck.

"But why would they want Burlington?" The Sheriff asked as he leaned against his horse, which then moved and rocked the Sheriff off balance.

"That is a question we can answer while we ride!" Hiawatha mounted his horse and took off.

All the posse jumped onto their horses and galloped for Burlington. They rode hard and the desert sand and dust bit their lips and parched their throat, but they kept on. Brock pulled his handkerchief out and tied it around his head. James thought as he rode, Dorothy was in Burlington, in that moment he wished he could sprout wings and fly to the town faster than the outlaws. He prayed that God would keep everybody safe in this hour of distress, whatever comes.

After half an hour of chase, the outlaws reached the one-mile mark and had the town in view; the Sheriff, Brock, Hiawatha, and James then knew that's where they were headed.

"What's the plan?" James shouted over the wind to Brock.

"Well I'm glad you asked! I think we should just walk in." Brock said matter-of-factly.

"Walk in? As in, walking. Like walk in?" James asked frantically knowing he had heard wrong. He sounded a little desperate in his voice.

"Walk in! The outlaws would take pleasure in letting us in; they'll take our guns and lock us up." Brock liked playing with James' smidgeon of gullibility.

"Brock, if I didn't know better, I'd say this desert sun has gotten to your noodle and fried off the end! Just walk in have our guns takin' away and then locked up! Sounds like you just made the day, Brock!"

"Well, you cut me short, only twelve walk in. Three stays out, after I see if this works I'll consider the rest of my plan."

"Look goofus-poofus. There are men's lives at stake. You can't just 'see if your plan will work.'"

Brock just remained quiet and turned to the Sheriff and told him the plan. At about a mile out of town and behind a big mountainside rock, the posse split off and Brock, James, and Hiawatha were chosen to stay out. The posse approached the town, and as they approached, they saw the outlaws stationed on house roofs, behind buildings, everywhere. James, Hiawatha, and Brock observed from a mountain above the town; everything went just like Brock had said. How did he know they would do that? The posse rode in and they were encircled by all the outlaws. Brock counted and all twenty-two outlaws where there.

"Brock, your skill is remarkable!" Hiawatha praised Brock, "James, should I go get fifty warriors?"

"We won't need 'em." Brock stated, not giving James a chance to reply.

"Umm, Boss says we won't need 'em." He acknowledged. "But what is next, Brock? Now that we got twelve men that can't defend themselves locked in the storehouse." They watched as each man was ushered into the storehouse, including a lot of the townsmen.

"What's the setup of the storehouse?" Brock wondered.

"Just two front windows and the door." James confirmed.

"Well this is the plan." Brock knelt to the ground, he made drawings in the dust of his plan of attack and then they sat back and waited for the night.

At dark, James and Brock headed for the marketplace, through the tiny back streets of Burlington, and without hardly any trouble made it there. They hid under a wagon and they watched the scouts as they walked back and forth in front of the store. A small candle burned in the store window. Their plan was to make it to the back of the store and go down into the cellar, then they would climb a ladder into the store. Hoping and praying that there would be no guards in the back of the store, they would then get all the rifles and all the ammunition they could carry, and head for the storehouse, distributing them out among the men locked up. James went over the whole plan in his mind repeatedly. Then when it was time to move they moved.

They crawled out from under the wagon without a sound; their boots dragging in the dirt. And silently, made for the back of the marketplace. Each silent step they took sounded to each of them as thunderbolts as they plodded along, both telling each other to be quieter.

Within a few minutes, they got there, and found the door to go down. Brock and James, guns drawn and ready, hearts beating, slowly made their way down the steps and closed the door. The cellar of the store was in total blackness, a blackness you could feel, they walked one step at a time, dragging their feet across the ground hands in front.

"Wish I had a lantern!" Brock whispered through the dark, which spooked James.

After a while of searching, they found the ladder and James cautiously creeped up to crack open the hatch and see if the surroundings were ideal for their next move. He watched for a while, and when all looked fine they started moving again. The creaking hatch was very loud and shook James every time he budged it a little farther open, in measured beats. Finally, they jumped out of their prison and found the guns, they were happy to see them; for they had not known if the outlaws had taken them or not. They had made straps to bind about ten guns together, then they searched for ammunition.

Suddenly, a match was lit on the other side of the room, next to the candle. James grabbed Brock's arm and told him to stop. They froze in their tracks, not making a sound. The match moved a little, and after a while burnt out and was relit. It got closer and closer, until they could see the man; he was tall and strong he had a long black beard, and it had looked like he had just got out of bed. They watched him grab a bottle and trot back to where he came from then the light went out.

"Whew! Safe?" James asked Brock, right over his shoulder.

"I think so." He whispered; but not certain.

The two got the ammunition and started back down the steps. They made it to the cellar door and out into the clean fresh air of the night. They walked with their heavy bundles from building to building, till they got to the storehouse. They watched the two guards' pace back and forth in front of the storehouse.

"We've gotta get rid of them. But how?" James wondered, waiting for Brock to come up with a plan.

Brock laid the rifles down he was carrying and walked closer to James.

"I'll bring them over here...when you get your chance, knife e'm!"

"Oh sure, just easy as that." James said mockingly, but at the same time, he knew that it would more than likely turn out just fine.

Brock pulled his hat lower, and drew his hanky over his face a little, took off his buckskin jacket, and then walked out into the middle of the street, staggering like he was drunk.

"Saayy! Friends, 'General' says it's my turn to watch but we can have a little drink together before I must stand guard. You need some refreshments, do you not?" Brock held a bottle up, "Where did he get that?" Thought James as he watched Brock acting like a total idiot. That was one thing he knew about Brock he didn't mind being the idiot.

The men started walking to Brock, they agreed, and Brock led them right past James. James threw two knives and they fell, silently; and nobody was the wiser. They quietly slipped to the front of the storehouse.

"Sheriff, Sheriff Brown!" Brock quietly called out.

"Brock! What is going on?" The Sheriff and a few others came to the window.

Brock slid the rifles through the bars on the window the outlaws had put in.

"Rifles!" exclaimed the Sheriff. "How'd you get 'em?"

"Save that glory-story for later." Brock exclaimed. "The plan is at dawn there will be a ruckus in the center of town I'll call on them to surrender or die then all of you open fire at my signal. That's what I got planned at least. Got that?"

"You bet'cha!"

Brock and James snuck back out of town and then James suddenly, stopped.

"Why'ja stop?" Brock asked as James came to a halt, bending over hands on his knees catching his breath.

"You go ahead I'll catch up!" James told Brock, and Brocks' eyebrow went up.

"Why would I go on? Or better yet why would you stay?" Brock pointed at James.

"I got somethin' to do." James trying to avoid telling him what his true mission was. "It's just something I promised somebody I'd do, and I have to do it!"

"Yeah I know how that goes!" Brock said his eyebrow still up gazing at James. "James remember before we left your house I had something to tell you."

"Yes!"

"Well I was gonna tell you, that there's a couple of men that—" Just then an owl flew low and hooted as it flew by, and spooked Brock and the story ceased for a minute. "Aaaah! Look at that! Look at that! Not even the birds of the night let me tell my gossip...I-I mean story. Lord knows I speak the truth."

"There's a couple of men that what?" James asked not even considering the interrupting owl.

"Well, they are the men that ruined your life, that are on your list to kill. And they are part of this gang that now has this town." Brock stated.

"But how do you know?" James asked.

"I found out." Brock jumped on his horse. "Meet you at the campfire. Be back soon, so I know your still kicking."

"I will" James tipped his hat mockingly to Brock, staring into the unknown thinking about Brock's last words.

James then slowly walked back to the town, he had to check on somebody. He made his way to the light green house, he approached the back of the house, to avoid the sneaky eyes of the outlaws. The Sheriff's house was dark, no lights shone in the dwelling. James then was spooked, he tried to open the office window, but it was locked. He went window to window, finally he came across one that was not. Unfortunately, it was the kitchen window, above the sink. He crawled through the window slowly, the kitchen was dark, and the window was small. Finally, after a little bit of extreme wiggling on his part, he stood on the floor inside the house. He stood there for a minute listening for a sound. As soon as he felt no unwelcome visitor was in the house, he slowly walked toward the living room; his boots sounding loudly on the wood floor. Just then, with gun drawn he came around some curtains.

"Drop your gun, or I'll shoot!" Came a soft but yet absolutely threatening voice from the darkness.

James instinctively jumped behind the wall. After a couple of seconds, he realized who it was.

"Dorothy, it's me! James!" He stayed behind the wall making sure she understood.

"James?" She slowly came walking out of the darkness. James watched as his beautiful fiancé, came walking into the light that shone from the moon into the room through the kitchen window.

"Yes! I'm here." James confirmed, holstering his pistol.

"Oh my! What's going on?"

"The group of outlaws we were chasing fooled us and took the town before we could stop them. Me, Brock, and Hiawatha are hiding in the mountain, and in the morning we gonna start a shootin'! You have to be hidden, out of the way of stray bullets. Do you understand?"

"Where are you going to be?" Dorothy asked more than worried.

"I'll be fine, remember I'm "Fast James'." He winked at her and started for the window. He got his legs through and was on his way down. He was almost all the way out, when a bullwhip went flying across his back, he cringed in pain, and fell to the ground.

"James!" Dorothy screamed quietly as loud as she could.

"Quiet Dorothy!" He jumped up, the outlaw man was getting ready for another swing, he swung his whip. James dodged and caught the thong of the whip, he cringed deeply at the sting of the whip as it wrapped around his arm. He pulled on it, and the outlaw came flying forwards, James punched him senseless, and he fell to the ground. James knifed his foe and kept going as if nothing had stopped him, waving goodbye to Dorothy who was still there.

11

"How'd it go?" Hiawatha stood to his feet. He and Brock were sitting by a small fire Hiawatha had made, situated behind a big boulder standing out of the mountainside hidden from the town.

"Better than anything I have ever seen. The Lord was surely helping us." James announced as he threw his leg over his saddle and slid off his horse. "By the way, what sort of a ruckus you planning for tomorrow?" He asked Brock as he pulled off a piece of the prairie dog Hiawatha had cooked.

"I'm not sure yet, I've thought about just walking in and beginning a fight, but then I'm in the crossfire." As Brock loudly chewed his food, he thought about what they would do next.

"Yeah wouldn't wanna be in the crossfire! Well I'm gonna go to sleep, you think and tell me when you gotta plan." James said as he unhooked his saddle from his horse.

"No, friend James, I think we'll leave you here if you're not awake." Hiawatha laughed, then he himself turned over away from the fire, leaving Brock to do all the thinking.

"How do ya like a fella like that?" Brock muttered.

James even though he laid there, he could not sleep. Thoughts of how they were going to get out of this kept running through his mind. He thought of Dorothy hoping that she was still safe. He thought of their new life together, hoping that that time would be soon. He then thought of his life's mission, to kill the men who murdered his family. From what he remembered there was three left, his mind seemed to cloud and blur every time he thought on this subject.

As he lay there, staring into the billions of unknown stars, he thought of his mother. She had died in childbirth, but before she died she had told him, "Faith is seeing light and love with your heart, when all your eyes perceive is gloom and despair." He had always stored that little verse in his heart, but it was only then when the full meaning of it came alive. Even though he had lost his whole family and bore the sorrows and gloom of that road. He knew deep down in his heart, that they were forever at rest; he had faith and believed that he would see them again in heaven.

As he lay there staring into the galaxies and the marvelous wonders of the sky, with both hands behind his head. He thought about what heaven would be like. In heaven, no more sorrow, no more pain, suffering, and death. No outlaws to chase, no murderers would run down those streets of paved gold.

But even at a different angle, a step out of his own realm, an imagination that he had never thought of; he thought of how really small he was, and a God that is so big. A God who stood back and spoke everything into existence. He thought of it, "Let there be light", and there it was. A God who created the heavens and the earth, every animal, every person, every ocean and river. And at the same time sent his only begotten son into a world he created. Sending his son to die, so that his creation, mankind, would have provision for repentance and live forever with him in heaven. He thought of God, sitting on his throne, a judge, a ruler, a King, knowing that he knew and cared for James Cassidy. He woke from his trance, and he prayed that God would direct his life, and the next day's events, and safely restore Burlington.

Around midnight, Brock stood up and walked to the top of the mountain and looked over and gazed on the little town. James saw him leave and followed him, he walked up silently behind him. "Stranger?" James asked jokingly as he stepped a little closer.

"Ha! I didn't spin around and almost kill you this time!" Brock chuckled.

"You're thinkin' about tomorrow?" James asked as he stood next to Brock and looked over the mountain side. Burlington had a few lights in it, the outlaws had evidently ceased their partying and took to sleep.

"Yes, and havin' a little difficulty at that!" Brock pulled on his beard.

"Well, I just wanted to come over and tell you before the big day tomorrow, I'm getting married after all this is over," he stated as he held his thumbs in his gun-belt.

"Let me guess...Dorothy Brown!" Brock guessed, his all too familiar smirk painted across his face.

"Uhh...yes, how did you know?" James asked, thinking he was not supposed to know.

"How did I know, Haahaha, that's a good one!" Brock chuckled to himself.

"Ahem, Well back to tomorrow; what's the plan? Assuming you have one." James quickly changed the subject.

"Well, I gotta say it's a little tricky; but here's what I had in mind." Brock sat on a log next to him and pointed towards Burlington. "What do you think would satisfy the robbers more than anything?"

"Seems to me your trying to get at something."

"Gold!" He answered with a little taste in his voice. "Gold. If they got their hands on some gold, why that would bring the whole outlaw gang to the center of town which gives the men in the storeroom a shot."

James just stared at him, his chin on his hands, his face displayed mockery. "And where in the world are you gonna get this gold?"

"That could be easily answered if the owners let us." Brock drummed his fingers on his knee.

"The-the Indians?" James started back in amazement. How could Brock even think of such a proposal? They had just been able to bring Hiawatha back into his tribe because of that very reason. "Brock, what in the world are you thinking?"

"We just need enough to make it attractive to the greedy outlaws, then we could return it. It would take us four or five hours to go, get it, and return."

"Now you two fellas stay fixed right where you are!" Came a voice from behind. They spun around pistols in their hands; a mean and cruel young cowboy stood in front of them, his hat was tattered and torn he looked as if he had travelled far. "I wouldn't do that, you see this gun here doesn't take kindly to staring down the barrel of another, it gets kinda nervous. And I don't blame it. Drop your belts." Brock and James dropped their belts and threw them down.

"What do you want?" Brock angrily asked. He was so mad, he hated the thought of listening and having to obey someone who held a gun on him.

"That gold you were talking about. You see I have travelled my life long and haven't touched a morsel of gold. And now you are going to bring me to that gold."

"That is something you're gonna have to talk to me about!" Hiawatha appeared behind the man and said in a commanding tone. The man whirled around to see his other opponent, Brock and James saw their opening and jumped on the man and he was down in seconds.

Brock stood the man up and went to turn away, but then recalled his job was not finished and he walked back to the man. "Now I will ask the questions. Who are you? Where did you come from?"

The man did not speak; "Alright you won't talk well we'll have to make sure you stay put. Hiawatha get some rope and tie him to that tree. We can't have interference into tomorrow's work." Hiawatha ran for the rope.

Minutes later... "Come on now get your hands up!" From behind them again, came a soft, but yet audacious voice.

They whirled around; and there stood a business man, he was tall and had a stupid face, he wore a gentleman's suit, a small mustache and had a small black derby hat. Four men stood behind him their guns drawn. But the man's form and his appearance, awoke James to the impending truth, he was the Frederik of that fearsome night. He grew red and clenched his fists but kept calm; he looked over at Brock. Brock had his face down as if not wanting to be recognized by the invader. But Brock was just wondering the same thing, he questioned if James recognized the man. He did not want Frederik to recognize him, for if he did, first he could be killed where he stood, and second, he knew James would find out his secret. They dropped their gun-belts again, after Frederik got two men and ordered to disarm them. They were led about two hundred feet away from the town and tied to two trees about five feet away from each other.

"Well we did good, didn't we?" James mockingly stated, when the men walked off after tying them; and then in a more somber tone. "That was another murderer, wasn't it?"

"Yeah it was, he was one of the leaders of the gang." Brock stuttered as he spoke.

"I vividly remember him arguing with somebody, but I can't just remember who. I know he's number five on the list, but that's all I can remember."

"Oh yeah?" Brock squirmed in his ropes as he listened to James.

"At least we got Hiawatha still out there." James announced through the darkness.

"No, you don't." Hiawatha approached in between two rough cowboy outlaws.

"What in the world? Hiawatha!" James jerked himself in frustration.

"I just came happily bouncing over the rocks with my rope, coming back to bind the first intruder, and I didn't see these rascals; they jumped me. Ask him," Hiawatha pointed to one of the men. "I gave him a punch he won't soon forget." After that the man slapped Hiawatha with the back of his hand. His head flew back, his hair falling in his face. "I told you." Hiawatha confirmed. He was tied to the tree and the men left.

James, Brock, and Hiawatha stood there for hours; by four o'clock in the morning, their feet hurt, and their backs ached. It was then when Frederik approached with five men.

"I was told that we captured an Indian, I wanted to see him for myself. You see, our work that we do entails collecting Shoshone, Blackfoot, Crow, and Apache scalps."

"You filthy murdering butcher!" Hiawatha jumped at the ropes that bound him, he stared at the man in the fire light; and knew the man as the man of his childhood, the man who he remembered had tied him up, and this man personally gave him the knife that he wore next to his side.

"Hahahaha. That's what they all say!" Frederik mocked Hiawatha.

"And this is what I say to you, you filthy deceitful frightful squaw. I am a man in my father's house, the next chief who will take my father's place. And I will kill every white man who ever thinks of stepping foot in our lands, and those who try to kill us, I will kill you."

"Am I scared of an Indian boy? Your whole tribe couldn't stand against my thirty men!"

"Do you wanna see an Indian fight? Untie me, I will fight five of your men including you, single handedly with only a knife, the choice of weapons is your own for yourselves. For if I die today, I will die with honor and with the favor of the great spirit. If you have the guts."

"U-Huh! Your challenging me to a fight, because I mentioned some scalps."

"You are scared! There is also a much deeper purpose for me killing you, and when it comes time for me to kill you, I will let you know my purpose for bringing your miserable life to an end." Hiawatha spit out his response.

"Hahahaha! You love your people that much, well I will grant you your heart's desire. You will die. You see, our plan is to attack the Shoshone camp in two days, we meet our friends down below in the morning. Yes, everything will work out just fine."

He tapped his knife on his hands coolly, he sheathed it, and took off his coat and vest, rolled up his sleeves, and walked up to Brock. "Brock!" He screamed in surprise and an evil smile spread across his face. "Fortune has brought Brock back to us. So, they let you out of jail, murderer? Hahaha!"

"Frederik your judgment days a comin', and you're gonna stand before the almighty, guiltier than the old angel Lucifer himself." Brock calmly stated under his breath, but with boldness none the less.

"That's what they tell me!" Frederik replied with a little laugh. "But you know I'm not as scared as you might think." James thought the two together reminded him of something; almost as if he remembered once these two men before arguing, but it was a memory off in the distance and out of reach.

One of the men standing next to Frederik, walked over and cut Hiawatha's ropes, and gave him a knife. "Hiawatha don't do it; you'd only get killed!", James pleaded. "Patience, brother!" was his only reply.

Hiawatha rubbed his wrists where the ropes had cut into him. He stood and looked at the six men who he had chosen to fight by himself. His mind raced searching for a plan, and before three seconds were up he threw the only knife he had at the man that held the torch, the man grabbed his chest where Hiawatha had thrown his knife, he crumpled to the ground and the torch that he had in his hands hit the forest dirt ground and plunged the woods into total blackness.

The remaining five drew and fired, not being able to see they missed him. They ran to the nearest tree or bush to hide. There they sat, the woods in total darkness, waiting. Minutes passed by and nothing happened.

James asked through the black. "Where'd he go?"

"And you're askin' me? How should I know." Brock replied with a little abruptness in his tone.

They sat quiet not a sound in the dark woods, a menacing silence spooked the outlaws as they sat staring into the unknown. Ten minutes passed quietly, with no sign of battle or Hiawatha. After another ten minutes, James felt a tug on his ropes.

"Hiawatha!" James whispered not seeing his liberator.

"Yes, here's your guns and your knife I went down to their camp killed their only guard and then got your weapons; and an extra knife." He added with a smirk. "Now ya'll go worry about Burlington; I'll keep these rascals at bay."

"We will stay here until we know you are safe." James said "We will stay in the shadows until it is over. And that is final!" James announced in a little more than a whisper.

"Thanks brother." Hiawatha put his hand on James shoulder. James shuttered when he felt Hiawatha's hand: it had the notion of dread and fear. Hiawatha then took off into the dark. They sat there quiet and listened to him trot off. The outlaws heard his walking and started shooting, but Hiawatha dropped to the ground and started crawling to avoid the bullets. They stopped shooting and Frederik started calling to Hiawatha.

"Look Indian fool, I don't have time for these cute little games. Now- "

He stopped for in that minute a blood curdling scream came from one of his men; casualty number two. He squirmed as he stared into the indefinite blackness of the night, not knowing where his pursuer really was.

Just then a scuffle, and then another moan, and a crumple to the ground. Frederik called out to Hiawatha to call off the fight; but no answer – just another man crumpled to the ground. There was no wind or sound in the woods to stifle the intimidating sounds of a man dropping to the ground with a moan.

Suddenly, in the dark forest came the noise of a fight, but this time they were both keeping each other at bay, struggling and muttering to each other, the noise of a battle. Then there was a moan, then an angry yell, a dying scream, and a crumple to the ground, then all was quiet. Frederik counting down, and knowing his time was coming, swore he would not be caught off guard. His gun in hand and a knife in the other, he put his back to a tree and stood there ready when he heard the call.

"Frederik!" Hiawatha screamed, there was a gurgle in his voice, and he was panting hard. He had returned to the place where he had left the six men. He had a cut above his right eye, where he had struggled with one of the outlaws. He relit the torch and set a small bush aflame to light the woods up.

"What do you want, Injun boy?" Frederik questioned from the darkness.

"Are you man enough to come out and fight me man to man? Or are you a little weak and frightened dog?"

"That is something I believe you will regret." He pulled out his knife and charged Hiawatha. Hiawatha jumped back to avoid the knife but tripped on a branch and fell to the ground. Frederik seized this moment and flew onto the Indian, one hand squeezing Hiawatha's neck another pulling down his knife to kill him, Hiawatha with all his might keeping the knife away from his chest. James could not stand any more of this for a second, he threw Frederik off of the now spent Hiawatha. James grabbed him by his shirt, jerked him to his feet, and in the stomach punched him, and punched him, and punched him. At the last punch James hit him in the jaw, Frederik went flying through the air, and lay motionless in the dirt.

Brock ran and knelt down beside Hiawatha, and it was then and only then when he noticed a knife sticking out of Hiawatha's stomach. He had taken on Frederik with a knife in him. "Hiawatha, speak, come on boy, answer me?"

Brock tried to get him to speak; but he was unconscious. James stood Frederik up, took his gun and walked back to Brock, and then noticed something was wrong. He saw Brock leaning over Hiawatha, nudging him as to try to wake him up, he saw a knife protruding out of Hiawatha's body. He ran and fell down beside Hiawatha.

"Hiawatha! Hiawatha, please answer, please!" James hysterically called out to his friend.

"James, he's just unconscious." James quietly knelt there and stared at his friend, his brother, laying on the ground blood flowing from his wounds, Brock was doing all he knew to do with wounds and keeping an eye on Frederik.

In that somber moment, with Hiawatha's head in his right arm, James reflected back and remembered his first encounter with his friend, he remembered how he saved his own life in the gunfight with Leonardo, he thought back on the day when they two became brothers by the custom of his people in the woods of the Whitmyre ranch, he would give anything for that day again. He remembered his acceptance back into his tribe and how his father's heart was glad. Tears streamed down James face as he thought on these things. Hiawatha began to open his eyes, he looked up and saw James, tears in his eyes. He glanced at Brock, he turned his head and saw Frederik standing with all but a smirk on his godless face.

"James." Hiawatha pulled at James arm. "Kill that man fo- for- he is th-the man who forced me t-to tell about my people's secret, give him this knife, James; point first!" He slowly patted a knife by his side.

"Not so, Hiawatha for you shall kill him." James said although in tears, trying to soothe his dying friend.

"No brother y-you do it for me. James, I have faced death twice now; when it was only one more second away the first time, I was not ready to meet my Creator, the second time, I am ready to meet my Savior. I took your bible one day and read a few verses, the only verse I was able to remember was. 'Your people will be my people; and your God, my God.' And that's true for me!"

And with that Hiawatha went limp in James arms. With a gentle caring arm under Hiawatha's head, James clinched his fist, his muscles tensed up, as he gritted his teeth and his whole body began to tremble and to shake, as if he were afraid. But it was not fear that shook this young man; it was the rush of adrenaline provoked by his red brother's lifeless body that made him stand up and face Frederik. No man living knows that feeling that young James possessed. James laid Hiawatha's head gently on the ground and looked up at the morning that had just started to break, great heavy sobs came through his chest. He looked towards heaven and gave a small prayer that God would help him in his next combat with Frederik. He slowly pulled the long knife from Hiawatha's sheath. He gripped it firmly and quickly spun to face Frederik.

With a tear stained face and adrenaline running sky high, he stared at Frederik. "Do you know who that Indian was?" James asked Frederik, as he pointed to the dead Hiawatha.

Frederik began to chuckle. "Humph! Why should I care? Dogs are dogs doesn't matter what breed they are!" Frederik laughed, and James found an opportunity and slugged him in the chin. "Now I'm done with you hitting me around little kid!" Frederik went to lunge for him; but as he was coming in, James dropped Hiawatha's knife he was holding by his feet, for he was not ready to kill him. James clasped both hands together and threw his clenched fists up with all his might, hitting Frederik under his chin, which sent him flying backwards.

"I wasn't finished talking, you filthy murderer!" James spitted out his response. "Does this look familiar?" He held up the knife and Frederik face glared dare. "That Indian is the same Indian you and another man forced to show you where the gold was on the land of the Indians. Here is that knife you gave him that night, and I swear that I will kill you with it this day. Point first! But I reckon not only that is against you, ten years ago around the same time, you tore up a little farmhouse, murdered the residents and burnt the house to the ground. That was my family, you ruthlessly murdered, you and four others and now for the honor of my family, of Hiawatha my Indian brother, and for the greater glory of God. Aahhhahh!!"

James jumped onto Frederik with the knife. As James descended, Frederik went to stab James in the stomach, but James punched his hand away, and sunk Hiawatha's knife deep into Frederik's shoulder.

With a cry of pain, Frederik turned and punched James in the chin. James went flying back, knife still in hand. He spun to avoid Frederik's knife, and then James screamed. "With this knife Frederik!" and plunged it deep into Frederik's chest. Frederik stood up, coughed, staring at James who had slowly backed up watching. Frederik whirled around and looked at Brock, then at the lifeless Indian, then squeezed his chest to try to stop the pain, but that was the last thing Frederik did on this earth, he dropped to the ground and died only a few feet from Hiawatha. Then James jumped up and ran up into the mountain alone and wept bitterly.

12

James ran and ran, till he could run no more and slumped next to a tree and cried. "God, why? Why? Why did Hiawatha have to die? Just a couple of months of friendship, vanished in a few seconds. He was my only friend and true companion. Why do you keep taking everything that I hold dear to my heart? God why?" He wept tears of sorrow and grief, until the light of day shone in its strength and brightness. He stood up, straightened his shirt, pants, and gun-belt, and prepared himself for the challenging day ahead of him. He went to the stream and washed his face. With every thought of Hiawatha, he had to keep from bursting again, but he had conquered his sorrow and had tried to resolve to turn his sights to Burlington and win.

He turned and looked at Brock who had snuck up to him. "It might seem strange or foolish, but I loved him as a brother." James told Brock almost as if he was admitting it.

"It isn't strange, James, you know I ain't a bible man, but I do know this that brotherly love is a strong force that is unquenchable. I think that's said somewhere in there."

"I don't know about that, but I do know it says. That life is but a vapor; it appeareth for a little time and then vanisheth away. I did not know that when I talked to him last, it would be the last time. I pray that when the time comes for me to die I would be ready."

Brock, a little uneasy, stood to his feet and approached James. "That was a long night I didn't get an ounce of sleep."

"I know." James looked at Brock, he had started to get suspicions about him. His face kept suggesting a nebulous memory to his mind that he couldn't recall with any clarity; a memory lost in the darkness of suppressed anguish. And then he wondered how Frederik knew Brock, it was all so strange.

"Well we can't go get the gold now." Brock mused, "Let's just go in and start the ruckus."

"I don't care...sounds fine to me." James answered just staring at the ground. Brock gazed at him, knowing that if he went in there with that attitude, he was going to get killed.

"James, your future is at stake right now. Look below at your town it is in the clutches of the enemy. It might be, that only we can save it. For the moment you gotta forget Hiawatha. That's what he would want. He wanted your town to be free. He joined the cause and marched with the posse. His love for you and your future would want you, for the hour, to forget and press on to free your town."

A little encouraged by Brock's words, James put his foot in the stirrups, slung himself on, tipped his hat and galloped away. Brock smiled as tears stung his eyes, for he too had missed the Indian that became their friend in the last few months. But even worse he knew the hour of truth was approaching. He mounted, and they slowly made their way down the mountain.

When they got within one hundred yards of the town's back entrance, they stopped and looked at the sun. It was about eight o'clock, and they took a few minutes to prepare for their attack. Then they split off; their idea was to attack single or double persons, single handedly without shooting, working their way to the storehouse to get the latest news and see if they were ready for the fight.

James immediately started out; he jumped over the wall and dropped to the ground. He paused listening for anybody, then he jumped from building to building, and to his surprise met or saw no one. He had made it within a hundred feet from the storehouse when a shot fired from above, hit the rock wall next to him, and shattered sparks and dust all over him. He dropped to the ground crawling for all he was worth, bullets whizzing all around him; the fight was on. He jumped up and turned down an alley. Two men were there running for him. They went to draw, but he drew first and dropped them dead in their tracks. He re-holstered and kept going as if nothing had stopped him. As the shots from above continued, he stopped behind a small post, barely enough to conceal him.

Just then he heard a blood-curdling scream. Startled, he looked up and a man was being thrown from the window. "Brock!" James thought to himself. He took the opportunity and ran for all he was worth to the storehouse. "Sheriff! Sheriff! You there?"

"No, we're in Guatemala hanging from coconut trees!" The Sheriff announced thoroughly annoyed as he came to the window. "Is everything gonna work?"

"We're gonna try to run 'em by here in a few minutes, when their perfectly in line start shooting." James ordered and not even waiting for a response, took off.

"Shoot! I was hoping to ask James for a piece of ham, or maybe even a small sandwich down from the---" The scrawny little town drunk began to ask. "Shut it up, little 'Wy-yi-outt'!" The Sheriff screeched out his harsh command. In the few hours he had been cooped up with him, he had begun a small personal detestation of the little drunk, for he had been the pest of the bunch. It was one thing to live in the same town as him but to be cooped up with him was another story.

James ran into the marketplace, it was occupied by four outlaws, he immediately jumped behind a pile of boxes. The men drew and gathered around the boxes, James quietly jumped on the wooden crates and waited; and they came around to where he could see them, "Ahoy!" he yelled. As they looked up they drew, and James fired and killed them. His heart had not forgotten his sorrows of the morning, but with every pull of the trigger and tread of his boots he resolved to free his town.

He leaned against the marketplace door, with the barrel of his pistol to his nose, smelling the gunpowder. He wondered what his next step would be, when a hand with a firm grip, grabbed his shoulder. He spun around and there was Brock. "You imbecilic fool! Why in heavens name would you come sneak up and grab me on the shoulder at a time like this?"

"The story of my life! I always scare people, including myself." He added.

"How many have you eliminated?" James asked hoping his number would be superior to Brock's number whatever it was.

"One." Brock said looking down at the four James had been able to kill.

"One?" James responded in shock. "Where you been?"

"I did just save your hide a minute ago." Brock said not sure if that would help the matter.

"One? Alright, Alright!" James replied. They stood in silence for a little while.

"We've gotta just run out. We gotta get to the storehouse, before everybody in the county knows were here!" Brock said.

James rolled his eyes and turned to face Brock. "What do you think I've been doing? I totally went to the storehouse and found out that everything there is still as planned, they still got their guns and their ready."

"Really?" Brock asked not sure where James was the whole time.

"Yeah, really!" James slapped Brock's back and walked out the door cautiously. As Brock went through the door, he looked up towards the sky, hoping that the good Lord would keep a steady eye on them.

As soon as they stepped out, they were getting shot at, they ran and hid behind a water trough. Bullets flew all around them, a shot whizzed right past Brock's head and penetrated the trough. Water spewed out of the hole onto Brock's back, he jumped from the cold water that hit his back. They had to escape from the trough, the outlaws were creeping closer and closer and their shots got ever so nearer. At the count of three, they burst and ran into a building next to them.

Shots kicked at their heels; they searched for any way of escape, but there was none; they were trapped inside the building. They looked out the window and a few outlaws were working their way towards them, guns drawn. James and Brock let them have it, in unison they shot, a couple outlaws fell, another spun around and shot towards James. It hit the glass window and shattered; shooting fragments everywhere. James whirled around to avoid the erupting shards, but he was hit by glass fragments in his back and shoulder. His shirt torn, and his arm bleeding a little, he stood and looked at Brock.

"You okay?" Brock asked, glancing at James wounded shoulder.

"Yeah I'm fine. It ain't bad." He held it tight, to try to stop the slight oozing of blood from his shoulder.

James and Brock waited for other outlaws to show up, but they never did. After fifteen minutes of waiting and nothing happening, Brock and James decided to bolt and make for another building that at least had alternate exits. With guns drawn, they cautiously bolted into the open, running into another building, leading them ever so closer to the storehouse. The outlaws came filing towards them thinking they were trapped again, and this time they were gonna get rid of these invaders. But to their surprise dozens of shots came from the storehouse, leaving outlaws dead in the street, the battle had begun.

13

Brock and James were glad that they finally lured the outlaws to where the men could shoot from the storehouse. They refilled their pistols and prepared to push the attack even further. They looked up into a building and saw small puffs of pistol smoke in many places; the sound of gunfire was constant. The fervor of battle came over them, and soon they jumped out of their small prison, and ran into the open and quickly behind a trough, firing as they went. Brock kept going and jumped behind a wagon, James glanced over at him, he was already refilling his pistol.

The continued fire lasted for about half an hour, then all was quiet. Brock and James glanced at each other seeing if they were both still in one piece. After this assurance, Brock left for the building that had most of the outlaws hiding in. It was an old hotel, that was only used now for storage. James looked up and saw him go in. "Why in kingdom come, is he goin' in there?" he asked out loud, but no one responded. Brock made it to the door and crept in. Minutes later, he came running out and behind him a billow of white smoke; he ran over to James.

"Wha-What? Your gonna burn it down?" James asked frantically.

"No, it's just smoke, like a smoke signal. They'll show their nasty heads in a minute." Brock leaned against the trough, cocking his .45 colt.

"Smoke! Beats me you always have something strange up your sleeve."

"I've learned a few trades along the way. Fill a cook stove with a rug and pull the pipe, and light it. That's one way at least!"

"I see!" Their conversation was quickly ended, when out of the building the outlaws swarmed out.

Sheriff Brown was leading the men and was doing a good job at it. "Alright come on men, fire. GO!"

"Sounds like there's a small likelihood of somebody gettin' hurt. I ain't gonna do no shootin'!" The town drunk plopped down. The Sheriff had had his fill of being pinned up with this loud assertive mouth for a night and a day. With a glare in his eye, he grabbed a big pile of heavy dusty blankets and threw it on top of him. Finally, this drunk would be quiet, or was he. The little fat guy clawed at the blankets, and pulled himself out of them, coughing and sputtering and totally white with dust, he took on the Sheriff. "I'm a gonna get me myself a cheap lawyer, the cruelty that is displayed in here is shocking; and I will be satisfied." The Sheriff stared at him, then turned around and threw him a careless hand. "Aw!"

James and Brock were doing their best to keep the men moving towards the storehouse, but they slowly kept moving away, bullets whizzed in both directions. The citizens of Burlington were all laying on the floor, or in their cellar, away from the bullets that seemed to fly around every corner. After an hour of chasing and shooting they were finally able to walk in the center of town without being shot at; they considered everything to be fine. The men in the storehouse came filing out slowly, and each ran for their own house to see how their families were.

"Watch me." The dusty drunk unbeknownst to all that just took place, walked to the Sheriff and commanded. "Watch I'm gonna take this to court o'law. Yup, going right now. Watch!" He stumbled all the way to the courthouse and went and grabbed the door handle. He went to pull, and it was locked. Expecting it to open, his hand roughly slipped off the handle and hit him in the stomach. "Humph!" he grumbled. The Sheriff and James now laughing, and the old little town drunk just shrugged his shoulders and headed for the saloon.

Suddenly behind them gun fire started again, the Sheriff whirled around grabbing his shoulder, he stumbled to a tree and sat there. James dropped to the ground to avoid the continued gunfire, he crawled behind a large barrel, seeing the shooter, he gave two shots in his direction. The shooter immediately ceased firing; James ran to the Sheriff.

"You alright? Just looks like a graze." James said trying to comfort him as he held his aching shoulder, groaning.

"Yeah! And I'll graze him!" The Sheriff yelled standing to his feet; using the tree to pry up on. James helped him to his feet.

Just then as if it were a new band of outlaws, the small town became filled with outlaws once more. The sound of gunfire echoed through the streets, as James hurried the Sheriff to cover; he took him into a hotel where he could shoot from a window but was protected. The hotel keeper waved away James, letting him know the Sheriff would be fine; and James reentered the street.

The wind began to pick up, and dust and smoke filled the town. James watched the steady wall of outlaws; there were at least sixteen. Where did they come from? He thought they were killing them. But it was the reinforcements of Frederik they did not know were out there. He pulled some friends together and made a quick plan, not knowing where Brock went he thought he had to start thinking for himself.

"Come on guys! Let us weaken their line! Make sure your shot counts; after the first burst of gunfire, their gonna run. It's time to face 'em head on!" James quietly encouraged his men.

At James signal, his little group of five young men, fired; the outlaws started to panic, looking for a place to flee and hide. Townsmen returned back from checking on their families. Everywhere the outlaws turned they were forced back to the center; only eight outlaws were left standing, they were tightened into a tight ball of defense, where they still had their guns drawn. James and another young man slowly came out of their hiding place, to face them and ask them to surrender; James yelled out above the wind.

"I call on you to surrender. Your lives will be spared; throw down your weapons."

"We will not surrender!" One of the outlaws spun and shot the young man next to James. James at once shot the shooter in the head. The men next to the dying murderer shrank back but continued shooting. James pulled the young man to cover, and then took his position behind a post. Then the outlaws unexpectedly, laid on the ground prone, which made them more difficult to shoot; James went into the third story of a hotel and fired one by one until the last outlaw was left. The man dropped his gun and ran but was shot by a shooter on the ground.

14

James scanned the town's scenery; everywhere he looked, men lay in the streets. He saw a few townspeople lying dead or wounded; but more outlaws lay dead in the dirt roads. He removed his hat banged the dust off, thanked God for his protection and he sent a special plea to heaven to heal his town, Burlington.

Suddenly like the blow of a hammer, like the instant feeling of being stabbed with a knife; his eyes still closed in prayer, jerked open. For there was a blood-curdling scream off in the distance, of a familiar voice that came through the dusty, dry air. He jerked up his head and looked around. There down below, he saw it. A man was walking out of the church, a man that had a mean and cruel face, with a long scar down his left cheek.

In that slight second, as he gazed on the wicked face, he was enraged; a bitter hatred of the man and a memory ran through his body. But it wasn't just the face of the murderer that put 'Fast James' into this unexpected high gear, and it wasn't only the remembrance of what this man had done to his family ten years prior; but there held tightly in the outlaws arms, was... "Dorothy!"

James jumped up and ran for the stairs to the roof top of the hotel with all his might and power. That poor old outlaw messed up bad this time; and every remembrance of what he saw kept him running for all he was worth. It was the Travis of that horrifying night of his youth, and now the same Travis held his Dorothy captive, with a gun to her head trying to make his way out of town with a hostage, so he could be guaranteed safe passage. Dorothy frightened and scared, searched for James among the bystanders, but could not find him. The Sheriff watched from his window terrified, with his rifle waiting for an opening. Travis slowly backed up towards his horse, he was getting ready to mount, when from the church roof he heard a challenging voice.

"Murderer!" James yelled as he hit the ground gun drawn. "Drop your gun, cutthroat!"

Travis spun around and faced James; still holding Dorothy in between. "You better back off sugar! Yo mama sure don't wanna haft go to no funeral today. Ha, the funny thing is she might already have to, so it won't be that big of a bother. But I know this one thing is for sho, and I ain't sayin' it again, if you don't put that revolver down, this girl is gonna be was-was!"

"What do you intend to do with her?" James asked, gun still in hand but lowering slowly. His blood boiling to overflowing, but in brief, it didn't know where to spill.

"You see I'm gonna be gettin' outa here alive. And there ain't not a if, and, or but about it. I'm taking her with me, you can find her in Gamerco, New Mexico. I'm sure this pretty little thing will be hanging around the fashion shop, and if she ain't there, you might wanna take a peek in the morgue; she'll be in Gamerco though, one way or another. And I'm not telling you again, honey child, drop the gun." Travis tightened the barrel to Dorothy's head.

Enraged, James held his peace. "Alright." He let his pistol swing from his trigger finger, with his pistol still hanging, he slowly raised his hands as if he was surrendering.

"James! How can you do this?" Dorothy screamed, she could not believe James was giving up, she never knew him to back down from anything, or was he?

In a split second he glared at her and glinted his eyes to the left, it was all a matter of seconds, but she knew he was telling her to scoot over to the right as far as she could. She gently and unnoticed by the murderous Travis, moved slightly to the right, giving James a small opening.

"Dorothy. Smart people know when to surrender and when done is done." But in that moment, James spun his pistol on his finger and with his high, out stretched hand shot Travis in the shoulder.

With this sudden burst of action, Travis had no time to react to anything; he dropped his pistol and grabbed his left shoulder. Dorothy ran away from him, to James, but James motioned for her to get away because his work wasn't finished.

"Good work, James!" Brock came up behind him and congratulated him.

"Thanks, but I ain't done. I am confident that that's another filthy murderer." James pointed to the man starting to rise to his feet.

"Your memory is correct. I was gonna come remind you if you forgot!" Brock confirmed as he pulled his hat a little lower over his face. James noticed it, he watched Travis as he stood to his feet. Just then Travis noticed Brock;

"Brock! They let you out'a jail, are you still the world's hero? Yeah, General, yo'r sho' on the wrong side of this fight!" Travis announced as he gritted his teeth from the pain from his shoulder.

"Enough!" James screamed at Travis. "Pick up that pistol, and ever so neatly and gently set it in your holster." James commanded pointing to the pistol in the dirt, then he tightened his own gun-belt.

"What is this a duel?" Travis questioned his challenger.

"And your askin' me! You are guilty of not only murdering many people today, and throughout your life. But as long as I have lived, since I was ten years old, I have wanted to kill you. Ten years ago, you and others came in and ruthlessly murdered my family just out of this town a little ways. Shot my father down in cold blood, my sister killed many of your men before you finally killed her, and then ya'll burnt our home to the ground."

"Now hold up there, sonny child!" Travis held his finger up and pointed at Brock, "That man was there to!" James looked at Brock in disbelief, but at the same time knew it had to be true but didn't want to believe it. Travis rolled with laughter. "He deceived you? HAHA! He is a good liar! He was there, ask him." James just stared at him, and Brock's silence was enough.

James turned back to Travis. "All I gotta say is you're the man on the line right now, Travis; and you will die where you stand." Travis laughed. "Prepare to meet your creator! You only got a little bit of time left." James stared at Travis, with his hat pulled low, his hands shaking over the pistol, but ready and perfectly able. Travis eyes were cruel and scheming; his pistol was also ready and treacherous.

After a few solid seconds, Travis found out that James wasn't going to move or budge, he drew and fired. But as if he had not even fired at all, Travis stood there holding his chest. And in the last ten seconds he had to live, he cocked his revolver again and turning to his right, shot a small fuse, that James had not seen before, lying in the dirt. Which then lighted and started heading to a large building which was connected to the storehouse with all the dynamite and powder; Travis then toppled over dead.

James pulled his knife out and ran to the fuse, he quickly knelt down and cut the fuse which was only a few inches from the building and jumped back to where he was standing. But to his horror, the fuses weren't spaced far enough away from each other and it jumped to the other piece he had cut. James and Brock turned to run; but it exploded. Three explosions went off, throwing James onto Brock, they got up shaking the dust off themselves. James looked up quick to make sure Dorothy wasn't anywhere around, then it was through the dust, he saw Brock's shirt had torn in the explosion, revealing a necklace and the pendant, the silver skull.

All questions now erased forever, James had all the proof he wanted to kill Brock. The skull of that necklace hit him like a blow with a hammer. He stood and took a few steps back, his love for his family wanted to kill Brock, but something held him back, unlike the others he had stood in front of before.

"You deceived me! I knew you were shady as a triple tongued sidewinder since the day I met you!" James yelled at Brock with his right hand gripping his pistol handle firmly while in its holster. Dorothy stood with her hand to her mouth, not believing what she was seeing or even hearing.

"James, I was there, I was one of the outlaws." Brock silently admitted.

"Then you have stated it yourself, and let God be the judge." James stepped back a few more steps, pulled his hat low, and prepared to kill Brock.

"James, the reason I got caught in a gang of reprobates like these, was because at that time we were in a revolt against the Mexican government. I was on a supply train that ran through this town; bringing supplies to the rebels of Mexico. It was my job. I knew this whole time, that this would happen one day. I led you to each of the murderers so that you could kill them, and that so your family could be avenged. When

I met you at your place the first time, I was on a mission to kill those men myself. They lied about me, they said that I was the one that murdered your family, that I single handedly did all those abominable things. When five men lie in court against you, who is the stinkin' jury gonna believe? I spent ten years of my life in prison, and it wasn't until Ferdinand, another one of the outlaws that was in our band confessed, that I did not do any of the killin' or robbin' they released me. James you remember this necklace." He pulled his necklace off, holding the skull in his palm. "When I pulled you out from behind a pile of firewood, saving you from the fire and the murderers, you grabbed it and ripped it off my neck, I carried you out and set you in a wagon that was full of hay, and I carefully pulled it out of your fingers. I have only worn it to this day in remembrance of you, and in pity of the fallen. You can shoot me today, I have said my piece. I do admit to being there that night, but at least you've heard the truth of what happened."

James stood there in disbelief. It sounded true, but at the same time he had part of his body ready to pull out the revolver. He stared at Brock, fifteen feet away, as he remembered the four murderers he previously had killed; he recalled back their evil faces, and the smirks that spread across each of their godless faces. James looked into Brocks eyes, and even though his own was fierce and full of rage and vengeance; Brocks face showed pity, love, and sorrow. With his hand gripping his pistol, his arm kept starting to pull it out, but he would push it back in.

With the fierce war raging inside his mind, he shut his eyes tight. Tears of an unsure mind stung his eyes. But when he opened his eyes, he looked and saw Brock unbuckling his gun-belt and starting to mount his horse. In the moment, James thinking he wasn't finished, yelled to Brock.

"Turn around and face me!"

"James if you're gonna shoot me its gonna have to be through the back," he answered James as he glanced over his shoulder. He ever so slowly continued to climb onto his horse. Just then, before Brock slung his leg over the saddle, he heard a shot. He jerked and felt a numbness go through his body. He squinted his muscles tight, expecting pain; but nothing came. Then he was startled when he heard a crash, and he looked down at his feet. There lay an outlaw that had been poised to shoot him from the church roof above. He turned and gazed upon the stolid expression of the man who had just saved his life. Holding his smoking pistol limply at his side, without a word, James turned and walked away.

Brock squinted at the tears that came to his eyes, for in that moment, he not only lost James Cassidy, he lost his best friend. He jumped onto his horse and sped away never expecting to see Burlington again. James looked back at the galloping figure. He had the same feeling. He had come to like Brock Gilmore; and in his heart he knew he would see him again. In only a matter of hours, James had lost his friend, his brother, and almost his future wife. He had to find a place to be alone. He walked out of town, and sat on a fallen log and prayed for God's protection, for his wisdom, for his peace, and for his grace. He prayed until he fell asleep on the log.

15

He woke with a start. He had been napping for about half an hour. He looked towards the sun. It was around three o'clock; he got up and slowly walked to the place he left Hiawatha. When he arrived, he was glad Hiawatha had not been bothered by anything, he had laid him in a small cave like shelter. Now he had to bring Hiawatha back to his people, He slung him on top of Hiawatha's horse, with him securely tied to his own horse, he made his way for the Indian camp.

It was five o'clock when he finally reached the camp. He stopped by the creek, and just like Hiawatha had done, James put the blue handprint, the peace symbol of the Shoshone, on both horses. Then he bent down, taking his hat off, combed his hair back, and with trembling fingers painted his face the same way Hiawatha had done his own; blue stripes running down the sides of his face into his neck, while white dots scattered his cheeks and forehead. He was ready to walk into the camp and meet the chief with his deceased son.

He rode in slowly, the Indians looking at the living and the dead. Tears stung at his eyes as he saw Hiawatha's people once again. One young Indian girl, standing outside her tepee not even looking at the young cowboy, saw the fallen and screamed as she turned back into her tepee. By this time the whole Shoshone nation had come to see what had happened to their chief's son. When he reached the tepee of the great chief Washakie, the chief stood his arms folded and great sorrow spread through his face.

"Your son, my brother!" James said showing great sorrow as he spoke. "Your son's people were at stake and your son fought off every last one of the enemy..."

"That is enough!" The chief slowly interrupted James. "We will hear what happened at his funeral."

A great and terrible moan went through the Indian camp, everyone shared in their loss of the chief's son. Right at sunset, high in one of the Yellowstone mountains, the funeral ceremony began. Drums began to play, a slow and gloomy beat sounded through the assembly bringing every member of the tribe together. Around eight o'clock under a full moon, and with many fires, the family of the departed stood in a line, sisters, nephews, cousins, uncles, aunts, father, mother, all stood there as eight young braves carried Hiawatha on a stretcher, made with poles and buffalo hide. Hiawatha laid motionless a small indistinct smile spread across his face.

They continued walking right past the family, the last in line was Chief Washakie himself. When they approached Chief Washakie, they stopped, and stood there, they were standing in front of a tall platform at least twelve feet high. Then walking up a few steps they laid Hiawatha's body on top and descended once again.

The great medicine man of the Shoshone walked up with his shaker and reverberated through his deep voice, mutterings. After he had called on the great spirits to lower and take Hiawatha's soul away, he backed up and the whole Shoshone nation gathered in a circle around the platform and chanted the Shoshone funeral song.

While the singing began, many squaws came leaving flowers, food, and even clothes, for the long trip ahead of him. One young Indian girl walked up to the platform, with a somber and grief-stricken face, she had in her hands two white flowers that were tied together with the sinew of a deer, and after sitting there a few minutes she left the flowers and returned to the line. James stood next to the chief, his face paint smeared by tears which enhanced rather than diminished the symbolism of the blue stripes and white dots. Family. Unity. Love. Compassion. There was no better expression of Hiawatha's friendship and sacrifice. The tears welled afresh.

After half an hour of chanting, the Chief stepped up to speak.

"My people, we are a proud and free people. We are proud of our name, of our clans, and of our ways. My son even though apart is still part of us. He offended his people innocently, then came back forgiven and passionate. He died with renewed Shoshone fire and blood. James, a white brother to my son, will speak and inform us of how he died and what he did to be killed like this."

The Chief slowly turned to James. He motioned for James to come up. James walked up to the chief, and shook his hand, and looked at the crowd.

"I remember the first day I came to this Indian camp," He talked to the Indians gathered, some understood him, others could not. "I came and begged the chief to forgive Hiawatha, for he was a good man. He fed you, and you were happy. Well in the same manner, he died for his people. A group of five men, said they would come and kill many of you, for your scalps. Hiawatha for the love of his people, like a wild dog fell on them, killed most of them. One of them stabbed him, but still he fought on. Finally, after they were all killed, Hiawatha fainted and then died in my arms a little later. We did all we could for him, but he was gone. He died with honor, with dignity, and with heroism. My love for him and for every one of you is still the same."

He nodded to the chief, who had tears in his eyes. Even James as he told the story, had to bat his eyes with his sleeve. The crowd slowly walked away, and James embraced the chief. After talking a little with the chief, James set out on his way back home, carrying with him a tangible emptiness, like the darkness of a cave, and the image of a blue handprint engraved on his minds eye. The cost of peace etched into his soul; the bitter-sweet memory of a friend that sticketh closer than a brother.

16

A few weeks went by, and with the wedding of James Cassidy and Dorothy Brown coming up; the town felt like an organized city again. James put a corral up at his place and bought a few cows; making his place more like a family's homestead. He busied himself and anticipatedly waited for that day. Every evening he would go by the Sheriffs house and visit Dorothy.

Finally, the day came, it was a beautiful summer morning, flowers lined the pews, and an old man stood behind the pulpit preaching his wedding ceremony speech. The wedding ceremony went by very slowly it seemed, as the two sat side by side all the way in the front. After the wedding sermon, they rose and exchanged vows; they were glad and happy together. Now forever behind him the chase of murderers, he could settle down and have a family. His heart knew no other joy, than that he was partaking of that Saturday morning.

As he stood there, listening to the old pastor, he happened to glance back, and then his eyes caught a familiar face. All the way in the back stood a man in the doorway, with a suit and tie, shaved, and hair neatly combed. He glanced back again at the face, and his heart sorrowfully looked away for it was none other than his lost friend, Brock Gilmore.

He turned back to Dorothy and the wedding, and they both turned to walk out the church doors, with cheers and whistling and laughing all around them. He looked back at the door, but Brock was gone. He grieved in his heart, but Dorothy didn't know, for he was making the moment for her.

After a short honeymoon, James set out one early morning to look for a lost friend. He scanned the horizon, looking for a small campfire. But there was nothing. He searched all that day looking and trying to find Brock; but it was in vain. Finally, with the sun setting, he returned home to his newly-wed wife.

That evening as they sat in their porch swing watching the sunset, they heard the sound of a galloping horse coming towards them. They stood and walked to the end of their porch and waited for it to approach. James heart did a jump thinking it might be Brock.

As the galloping figure topped the hill, James recognized the rider as Hiawatha's squaw, she sat there examining the little house; and then rode down.

She rode up to the porch and dismounted, and walking up to the couple, knelt down, and began to untie something wrapped in deerskins. As she pulled it out she gently handled the contents. She then stood, and James remembered it as Hiawatha's warbonnet; it was draped over both of her arms. She looked up at the two, and with tears trying to start in her eyes; she spoke.

"This is Hiawatha's warbonnet. I believe that he wants you to have it: and it is also the wish of Chief Washakie!" She said and then jumped back on her horse and rode out into the growing darkness.

James and Dorothy stood on their porch and watched the figure slowly slipping away. With one arm holding the bonnet and one around Dorothy, James bit back the remembrance of Hiawatha and the pressing tears.

"Poor Girl!" Dorothy announced after a little bit of silence. "I was just thinking that could easily have been me. May we all have a better life after this!"

James fitted Hiawatha's warbonnet on and answered. "Yes...May we all!"

They turned and walked into their house.